"How, pray tell, did you intend to get these—" his sweeping glance encompassed the dozen bulky doll carriages "—from here to the party?"

"Don't worry. I'll call one of the engineers in the morning." Lucia rattled on without thinking. "The author of my book on how to get married would be proud of the way I can take a problem like this and turn it into an opportunity to meet a potential lifetime partner."

"A good way to meet someone?" he repeated.

"Well, yes. I mean, you have to approach these things logically." The man was a mathematician. He should appreciate logic. "The fact is, I have a dozen buggies to transport, right?"

He merely nodded.

"And I have no car. I *could* call a girlfriend from my section, right?"

"Good idea. Do that."

"No, no, no. I can kill two birds with one stone by using the company directory to call someone I don't know, some *male* I don't know, and get him to do it."

Daniel made a choking noise and began to turn red. "Miss Callahan, this is a data processing firm, not a dating service!"

Dear Reader,

Welcome to Silhouette—experience the magic of the wonderful world where two people fall in love. Meet heroines that will make you cheer for their happiness, and heroes (be they the boy next door or a handsome, mysterious stranger) that will win your heart. Silhouette Romance reflects the magic of love—sweeping you away with books that will make you laugh and cry, heartwarming, poignant stories that will move you time and time again.

In the coming months we're publishing romances by many of your all-time favorites, such as Diana Palmer, Brittany Young, Sondra Stanford and Annette Broadrick. Your response to these authors and our other Silhouette Romance authors has served as a touchstone for us, and we're pleased to bring you more books with Silhouette's distinctive medley of charm, wit and—above all—*romance*.

I hope you enjoy this book and the many stories to come. Experience the magic!

Sincerely,

Tara Hughes
Senior Editor
Silhouette Books

TERRY ESSIG

The Wedding March

Silhouette *Romance*

Published by Silhouette Books New York

America's Publisher of Contemporary Romance

For Peggy Parent.
Mom, men may be like streetcars,
and there may always be
another one coming along,
but the one I caught
was made by Cadillac.

SILHOUETTE BOOKS
300 E. 42nd St., New York, N.Y. 10017

ISBN: 0-373-08662-8

First Silhouette Books printing July 1989

Printed in the U.S.A.

Books by Terry Essig

Silhouette Romance

House Calls #552
The Wedding March #662

TERRY ESSIG

says that her writing is her escape from a life that leaves very little time for recreation or hobbies. With a husband and six young children, Terry works on her stories a little at a time, between seeing to her children's piano, sax and trombone lessons, their gymnastics, ice-skating and swim-team practices, and her own activities of leading a Brownie troop, participating in a car pool and attending organic chemistry classes. Her ideas, she says, come from her imagination and her life—neither one of which is lacking!

Chapter One

Lucia Callahan was so tired even her hair had gone limp. She blew a long blond strand back out of her eyes. She stared at the half-assembled plastic baby buggy in front of her and muttered in a mocking singsong voice, *Don't do things by halves, Lucia. That's the way divorce courts do it.* "Darn you, Mother!" she continued irritably in her own more melodic voice. "Look where your constant stream of proverbs has landed me now. It's way after hours and I'm alone in a deserted office building trying to put together doll buggies so that a bunch of kids I don't even know won't be disappointed at the company Christmas party tomorrow."

She could almost hear her mother's response. *Lucia, if a thing's worth doing, it's worth doing well.* "Oh, yeah? Well, *half a loaf is better than none*, Mom. At least the little twits are getting a free present courtesy of the Statler Club Santa." Lucia put a hand to her forehead. "Oh, Mom," she wailed. "I'm over a hundred miles from the diner on Route 29, hours from Chillicothe. But you might as well be right here in Chicago. All your obnoxious sayings are permanently etched in my brain!'' She held her head as if to ease the burden of the maternal maxims weighing her down.

After a moment, she sighed and raised her head. The half-assembled buggy stared back at her. Eleven more of the suckers waited in their boxes right behind it. She would be there all night. She gave the quarter in her hand an accusatory glance. Necessity might be the parent of her mother's inventions, but Lucia was unimpressed with her makeshift screwdriver. Grimly, she set back to work.

This whole mess was her family's fault anyway. Okay, so she'd been three months premature. That was twenty-four years ago, for crying out loud. Did they still have to be so overprotective? One more *look before you leap, Lucia,* and that leap would have been off the nearest bridge. So she'd occasionally bitten off more than she could chew. Nobody was perfect.

Lucia did her best to stretch the buggy frame, trying to squeeze the next piece into place. Five foot nothing was big enough for a woman. Heck, she only felt small and frail when she stood next to her parents or brothers. Who wouldn't? Even her mother was over six feet tall. There was such a thing as too much of a good thing, you know. Lordy, Lordy, this was getting grim. The older she got, the more she sounded like her mother. With a final exasperated tug, the piece popped into place and she went to work with her quarter.

Her three huge brothers had been as bad as her parents...intimidating her dates and setting her up with trusted friends who "respected" her to death.

The whole darn town of Chillicothe, Illinois watched not only over Route 29 as it wended its way along the Illinois

River and on into Peoria, but also over Lucia Callahan. Every move she made was reported back to her parents, Harvey and Edna, because Lucia had needed watching over. The entire population seemed to know she'd almost died when she was born.

In her heart of hearts, she knew she would never be accepted as an adult by her parents and their peers until she was successfully wed. Heck, her mother had *told* her she might as well paint a red *A* on her chest as move out on her own before marriage.

When she discovered the book *Finding a Man, A Girl's Guide to the Altar*, she knew her problems were solved. She took the book's advice very seriously and wrote out a list of what she was looking for in a man. For an organized person like Lucia that was an easy task. There was only one real prerequisite. She would find someone short to marry and teach her about life. Someone who wasn't afraid of familiarity breeding contempt, for she wanted to get familiar. Someone who believed in striking while her iron was hot. And all that added up to…someone her own size who wouldn't take one look at her and run to the nearest exit for fear of being cast in the role of the proverbial bull in the china shop.

The book had pushed her into this latest predicament. She'd left her position of nursery school teacher and moved to Chicago on its advice, for how could a girl expect to be caught if she swam where no one was fishing?

The book had a point. You weren't likely to rub shoulders with a lot of eligible bachelors teaching in a nursery school in a place the size of Chillicothe. So she went for computers. What could be better? An up-and-coming field, interesting and…lots of men. The fact that she knew little about the field was no deterrent to someone with ingenuity. She'd taken typing in high school—who hadn't?

And she knew her alphabet. So she took a clerical position in a computer company's personnel department.

Join clubs. And not the Ladies Junior Auxiliary. Clubs that cater to both sexes. Choirs, hobby groups, do-good organizations, sport clubs, but not PTAs.

She'd checked out the church choir, but there hadn't been anyone there younger than sixty. Lucia took on the presidency of the Statler Club instead. It was the association responsible for all company parties. It seemed perfect, for the young singles in the Statler Computing Group were the only ones with the time to donate. She would be gaining brownie points with the company higher-ups while mixing it up with possible eligibles. Perfect.

One last twist of her quarter brought the screw firmly into place and she moved on to the next.

In fact, two promotion parties and a bowling blast featuring pizza and beer had gone well. Then she'd bumped headlong into the dreaded Christmas party. The parameters were loosely constructed at best. The only tradition seemed to be the party itself. It was held at no particular place each year, just someplace big enough for 350 people. There had to be enough food to fill all those bodies, no particular variety; activities to suit both kids and adults, whatever caught your fancy; and presents in the ten- to fifteen-dollar range for 110 children between birth and age twelve, including a Santa Claus to pass them out.

Nothing to it.

The problem was, the parameters were so loose she was flummoxed. Should she offer a full meal or just hors d'oeuvres? A magician or a caricature artist? The Holiday Inn? The ninety-fifth floor of the Hancock Building? The Museum of Science and Industry with free tickets to the coal mine exhibit?

Life at the diner run by her parents hadn't prepared her for this. She'd been close to tearing her long blond hair out by the roots.

Piece by piece, the party had fallen into place. Adler Planetarium was available December 12, and they'd even provide a private viewing of their Christmas sky show. That would keep everyone happily occupied. A caterer would provide simple food that even children would like, and a downtown bakery would provide sugar cookies cut like bells and dusted with red sugar. Tom, who had the desk next to hers and was handsome but too tall to be considered eligible, would be St. Nick. That left only the presents. Every employee got a three-page list of toys to choose from for their kids. They were to check their choice and provide the child's name and age.

So far so good.

The system didn't actually fall apart until they got to the present wrapping and tagging stage. Each of her volunteer helpers took an age group and wrapped those gifts. She got the two-year-olds, twelve of whose parents had requested doll buggies requiring assembly. Tom, Lorraine and Phil told her she was nuts, to just wrap the boxes and let the parents worry about assembling them. But a former nursery school teacher such as herself knew the little ones would be disappointed with a pile of nuts, bolts and plastic pieces.

Concentrating on her work, her tongue held snugly between rows of white teeth, she didn't see Godzilla from the Deep enter the employees' lounge. The mountains of wrapped gifts ready for transport blocked her view. She didn't hear him enter the room, either. The sound of her own muttering as she tried to twist pink plastic flower screws into the sides of a buggy that had been purposely manufactured not to line up properly limited her ability to pick up sound. Godzilla finally tapped her on the shoulder to gain her attention, and she jumped a good three inches and dropped her quarter. "Darn it all," she muttered as the coin rolled on its edge in a lazy circle and disappeared under a low-slung couch. She looked up from her new position on her rump to blast the cause of this piece of bad luck.

She raised her eyes through yards and yards of what must have been a very expensive navy wool suit. It wasn't hard to tell. Its owner had put in a long day, for his tie was undone, his vest and jacket unbuttoned but still spread over alarmingly broad shoulders. There was an ink stain on the monogrammed cuff of his white shirt, but the suit still hung perfectly. By the time she focused on his head, her own was practically perpendicular to her body. This was one very tall person.

"My!" she gasped in wonder. Perhaps it would be best not to berate him too harshly for scaring her. Visitors in the building were required to show identification, but one could never be too careful. His suit spoke of quality, but she virtuously reminded herself that *you can't judge a book by its cover.* Then again, didn't *clothes make the man*? Too bad there was no time to call her mother and ask which was applicable here.

Godzilla tipped his face to look down at her. A new wave of emotions washed over her. His features were all blunt planes and harsh angles. They fit his massive body and the effect was of power and strength. He belonged on Mount Rushmore. His hair was dark and wavy, his jaw probably shaved clean that morning. His eyes were...indeterminate, at least from this distance.

"What are you doing alone in the building at this late hour, miss?"

"Uh ... just wrapping the last few gifts for the party to-morrow.... It's Mr. Statler, isn't it?" It had to be. No one else with the aura of power he had would survive without being the boss. The real head man would have fired him in an instant out of self-preservation.

It was. He looked around, impatiently tapping a well-shod shoe. "And where's the rest of the crew?" he asked, lowering a hand from the heavens to help her up.

"They've done theirs, sir." Now that she could see his eyes, she noted that they were very unusual ... brown around the edges and blue near the pupil. They might have been nice eyes had they been teamed with a smile. "Uh, I was trying to put the doll buggies together instead of wrapping up the pieces, you know?" Of course he didn't know. The boss man wasn't married, or so she had heard. What would he know about doll buggies?

He sighed wearily. "Give me your screwdriver. I'll help."

Lucia blushed. It was difficult to be dignified when talking to an armpit. "I don't have one, actually. It was sort of a last-minute decision to do this." Her voice trailed off faintly and she stood there a little uncertainly for a half minute.

She got a grip on herself. She'd moved hours away from home to get away from size intimidation, and she absolutely would *not* allow this megamale to step into her absent brothers' role. Mr. Statler's attitude should be *nipped in the bud* for *a stitch in time saved nine*. She looked up at him and smiled brightly. "Well, if there's nothing else, Mr. Statler, I really should be getting back to work. There're eleven more of the little horrors to put together when I'm done with this one." With that, she dropped onto all fours and crawled away in search of the quarter under the sofa.

Flat on her stomach and one arm stretching blindly under the furniture, Lucia breathed a sigh of relief when she heard his shoes firmly pad away behind her.

She should have known better. Large people, at least those of her acquaintance, had some silly idea that brain capacity was related to body size. With that kind of premise, it would logically follow that large people needed to help, guide and protect the small people of the world. And as her brothers pointed out continually, things got done their way by virtue of the fact that they *were* bigger.

No more than ten minutes and one pink plastic flower screw later, he was back. She looked up from her crouch by the baby buggy, and squinted against the bright ceiling light. "I thought you'd left."

"Had this in my glove compartment." He held up a yellow resin-handled tool.

Sure. He probably kept tools in his car just so he could produce them on occasions like this and make some short person look bad. "Thank you very much. It was kind of you to take the time to bring it back in. I'll put it on your secretary's desk when I leave tonight." That should be plain enough to head 'em off at the pass. Rising from her couch, she held out her hand to accept the tool.

He immediately palmed it. "Why don't you just get the directions for me?"

Rats. She hadn't even hesitated and she was *still* lost. "Really, Mr. Statler, that isn't necessary. I can take care of this."

"How long for this one?" The man's facial expression hadn't changed one iota since he'd come back into the room. His granite face would probably crumble if he smiled.

"About forty-five minutes." She sighed impatiently. "But once you've done one, I'm sure the others will go faster."

"Two screws in forty-five minutes. You wanted these for tomorrow?" He arched an inquiring brow in what she was sure was a major effort for his facial muscles.

"I can—"

"Won't get anything accomplished at home knowing you're here. I'll stay. That way I'll be sure nobody's bothering you."

This was *worse* than back home. You could take money to the bank on a bet that nobody would bother her with Mount Rushmore at her side. "This really isn't necessary," she repeated, all the while knowing her words were falling on deaf ears. "There's a guard at the front door. Nobody can get in here without a thorough security check. Who would bother me?" If he could come up with somebody under six feet and halfway decent looking, she would consider bribing the guard herself.

He raised a second brow in the most facial expression he'd shown so far that evening. "You can never tell. Cute girl. Late night. Deserted building. Sleepy guard. It reads like a recipe for trouble. You've got to be new in Chicago."

She would kill him. He was purposely trying to scare her, just like her family used to do. Well, just as soon as she figured out a way to reach that thickly corded neck, she would absolutely strangle him. Lucia fumed as she watched him effortlessly pull open the heavy metal staples of the next carriage box and begin to extract the pieces. She turned back to her own instruction sheet. "How do you know I'm not from the city?"

"Besides the obvious naive behavior? Your *A* isn't broad enough. Close, though. Downstate?" *He* already

had the pieces of the base correctly lined up and was inserting his first screw.

Well, that was the easy part anyway. Wait until he got to
the screws that looked like plastic flowers. Ignoring his
questioning statement, she began gnawing her lower lip as
she concentrated on stretching the fabric liner over the
frame the way the hazy illustration seemed to indicate. One
screw through four layers was to hold everything in place.
But nothing fit properly. The four holes for the one screw
were off by a good half inch, and each one missed in a
different direction from its neighbors. Looking over her
shoulders, Lucia realized her boss had almost caught up to
her. He was already inserting a completed plastic frame
into the limp fabric liner.

Viciously, she forced the screw through the outside support and tried to pull the hole in the fabric closer to the
protruding plastic plug. The problem was her quarter
screwdriver. If she had proper tools, she could zip along,
too. She just hated it when her mother was right, but once
again she hadn't looked before she leaped and was stuck
with a lousy quarter and a lack of foresight. Now the inside strut had to be pulled the opposite way to get properly lined up and then the final fabric piece was stretched
down and—

"Oh, fudge!" she swore disgustedly. The quarter was
hurled into the sagging buggy, and she stomped, as much
as a ninety-five-pound person was capable of stomping,
over to the window where she folded her arms across her
minimal bosom and stared out into the winter darkness.

Daniel Thomas Statler's deep bass rumbled across the
room. "Problem?" he questioned.

She hated the way he spoke in shorthand.

"I put the pieces on in the wrong order."

"So reverse them."

She glared back over her shoulder and spoke distinctly. "They are irreversible screws and cannot be removed." She was careful with her pronoun, noun and verb. If she could have thought of a few adjectives more flowery than *irreversible*, she would have used them as well.

Daniel sort of grunted and looked at his own set of directions. Then he walked over to her sadly lacking project, carefully placed his screwdriver between the two supporting pieces of plastic and, with casual finesse, popped the screw loose without even the smallest tear to the fabric of the buggy body.

Daniel put together nine buggies in the time Lucia struggled through three. When he offered to help her load them in her car, he could tell by the dawning look of horror that she hadn't given the gifts' transportation a thought.

"What kind of car is it?" he asked fatalistically.

She blushed and mumbled, "Actually, I don't own one."

He sighed. It was enough of a wind to blow a few tired hair tendrils out of her eyes. "How, pray tell, did you intend to get these—" his sweeping glance encompassed the lineup of a dozen bulky doll carriages "—from here to the planetarium?"

It was poor form to rattle one's superior and she had done little else all evening. Lucia was quick to try and pacify. "Don't worry. I'll call one of the engineers in the morning." She rattled on without thinking. "The author of my book would be proud of the way I can take a potential problem like this and turn it into an opportunity to meet somebody new. Well, thanks so much, Mr. Statler. It's been a pleasure, but I've got to run."

It was a poor way to calm down a boss. He eyed her the way one would a bug in a cup of soup and crossed his arms over his chest. It was an autocratic pose she recognized immediately from her father. "A good way to meet someone?" he repeated questioningly.

Lucia backed out of his reach before responding. "Well, yes. I mean, you have to approach these things logically." The man was a mathematician. He should appreciate a bit of logic. "The fact is, I have a dozen baby buggies to transport, right?"

He merely nodded.

"I have no car." She licked her lips nervously, sorry she'd opened her big mouth. "Here's where the advice in my book comes into play. I *could* call a girlfriend from my section, right?"

"Good idea. Do that."

"No, no, no." Looking up, she smiled triumphantly into his face. "I can kill two birds with one stone by using the company directory to call someone I don't know, some *male* I don't know, and get him to do it."

Daniel had never ground his teeth before in his life. But he was close to it now. Very close.

"It serves two functions. The Christmas gifts get over to the planetarium, and I have the opportunity to make contact with a potential life partner." In her small-town naïveté she thought Daniel would be impressed with her reasoning processes.

Instead Daniel made a choking noise and began to turn red. He raked his hand disapprovingly through his hair and roared in clipped tones, "Miss Callahan, this is a data processing firm, not a dating service!"

Goodness, a compound sentence. Considering the terseness of his original conversation, she was impressed.

Lucia kept her distance while she earnestly argued back. "But, that's what is so wonderful about this. It can be both at the same time, don't you see? Approximately half of your work force is unattached. What could be more natural than for them to meet while taking care of the business of the Group?''

"No, I do *not* see, and no, it is *not* natural. It is cold-blooded and calculating to go blatantly gunning for a husband like this.''

Would he prefer she be underhanded and sneaky about it?

"Do you have some kind of scale to rate them all on so you can compare the candidates?'' By now his hair was sticking out in little tufts all around his head from being constantly agitated by his hand. She guessed it was the most emotion he'd shown in years.

"I would have thought a man of your background would appreciate a reasonable, rational approach to these things. Surely you're not waiting to be sprinkled with moondust or take one of Cupid's arrows in the buns to find your way to true love? One has to make one's own opportunities, Mr. Statler.'' She jerkily pulled red adhesive-bottomed ribbon bows from a plastic bag and stuck them haphazardly on buggy handles as she spoke.

Daniel grabbed up the stack of name tags and began attaching them. His jaw worked silently up and down for a few moments before he could speak. "I won't have the Group disrupted. Any good manager could expound for hours on the problems inherent in a company romance and I'll fire anyone who disturbs the swell we're riding right now,'' he warned, clearly meaning every word.

She sniffed indignantly. "If you're insinuating that I'm not pulling my weight around here, you couldn't be more mistaken. Look at my personnel file. I've gotten two raises in the short time I've been here because Ms. Thackeray doesn't want to lose me.'' She turned her back to aimlessly shift a stack of brightly wrapped packages while she rubbed salt in the wound. "Frankly, the kind of salary the Group offers its clerical staff doesn't exactly bring in the cream-of-the-crop type. You're lucky to have me. You get your money's worth. I just don't believe in letting God-given opportunities go to waste. I'll call someone in the morning. You'll get your gifts delivered and I'll get to meet an eligible candidate."

She began walking to the sofa in the reception area. Her coat was there. If she could get to it, now was a great time for an exit. He reminded her too much of her father for her to think he would let it drop if she stuck around. In a situation like this, clearing out was definitely the better part of valor.

She was sliding one slim arm down the lined sleeve of her black wool coat when it came.

It sounded simple enough. "Why would you want to get married in the first place?"

She shrugged as if it should be obvious. "I don't want to be alone anymore. I want to have someone of my own. Holidays to share, somebody to hold in the middle of the night. That kind of thing. Find out what all the fuss is about. See if two heads *are* better than one."

The big man studied her thoughtfully. "You're pretty young to be so desperate."

"I'm twenty-four and not at all desperate. I'm merely placing myself in a position of exposure. Remember the old saw about not putting your light under a bushel." She did the last black button and flung the collar cum scarf over her shoulder. She picked up her purse.

Daniel was shocked. He had assumed her to be right out of high school. Eighteen, tops. Twenty-four was a whole different story. She *was* cute in a wholesome, sweet kind of way. Feisty, too. But definitely playing with fewer than fifty-two cards. She could be a threat to his entire organization. "I'll have the maintenance men load the buggies into my car in the morning. You can ride with me," he informed her gruffly.

She stopped rummaging through her purse as she removed a four-by-six index card from its voluminous depths. It was an advertisement to share four tickets she'd been given to a concert. It would be nice if someone blue-eyed, male and short were to answer. Studying its wording critically for a moment, she responded absently, "No thanks. God-given opportunities like this don't come up every day."

It irked him that she wasn't even considering him as husband material. He didn't stop to think how truly irked he would have been if he thought some perverse female *had* set her cap for him. "You can pretend we haven't met yet. Tomorrow could be your big opportunity with me."

She gave him an uncertain look over her shoulder as she pinned her index card to the employee bulletin board, not quite sure if he was being facetious. "This is one conniving, marriage-minded wench you're safe from, Mr. Statler." She thought it safer to play it light. "You haven't got the one cast-in-cement nonnegotiable item on my shopping list." It was fascinating to watch the white shirt stretch and pull over massive pectorals as he shrugged back into vest and coat.

"And what might that be?"

"You're not short."

"Short?" he questioned disbelievingly. "You want to marry a midget? Whatever for?"

Lucia paused in the act of stepping over the threshold. "Why, so we'd fit," she pointed out kindly. "You're way up there while I'm way down here. I don't think we'd be very, um...compatible at certain times. Good night, sir."

So they wouldn't fit together, hmmm? Wouldn't they just. With that as food for thought, he pulled the knot of his tie back up his neck and went to check out the employee bulletin board. He read her card disbelievingly. This was probably another of her harebrained formats for meeting eligible males. Must not have lived in Chicago for long at all.

The card folded and carefully pocketed, he detoured past the personnel section, where he pulled one Lucia Marie Callahan's employment folder before flicking off the main lights and leaving for the night.

Promptly at nine o'clock the next morning, and just as Lucia had chosen one Harding, Thomas L., senior account representative, Area 2, as a likely candidate from the employee directory, three men from building maintenance descended on her desk like seven-year locusts.

She set the phone back in its cradle before dialing, as Frank, whom she had befriended almost on her first day a few months ago, spoke. "Hiya, Lucia. What d'ya know?"

"I know the sun's up because I saw it rising. But it isn't doing much to warm my day." She nodded politely to the other two whom she did not know.

"Ain't that the truth. But here's some news that'll warm the cockles of your heart."

She responded uneasily. "What might that be?"

"Ah, you probably already know." His cigar waggled suggestively up and down his mouth as he spoke. "You've caught the big man's eye. That should make you happy. Hell of a guy."

Flushing, she answered, "I'm sure I don't know what you're talking about, Frank."

Now his eyebrows waggled along with the cigar in true Groucho Marx style. "Sure, sure. All I know is I'm supposed to help these two guys—" he indicated his gray-denim-jumpsuited companions "—load the Christmas packages down the hall—" a finger pointed in that general direction "—into Mr. Statler's car *and* tell you to be ready by ten o'clock. He said he wanted to leave in plenty of time. And that there's always a lot of last-minute arranging to be done at a time like this. That's what he said. So I tell myself. This is it for Lucia, you know? Her chance at the great kahuna. I mean, why mess with the little fish in the pond when you can have the kingfish himself? Yes, sirree." He looked very pleased and Lucia cringed as the other two men took in the entire conversation. Discretion was evidently a foreign word to Frank.

"Actually, that won't be necessary, Frank. I'm terribly sorry Mr. Statler has put you out unnecessarily, but I was just about to call someone to come help."

It was true Lucia had occasionally asked Frank about some of the men on the staff before accepting any dates, figuring she didn't want to be bothered with a man who couldn't be nice to everyone. But when he leaned over her shoulder and inquired chummily, "Oh, yeah? Who'd you have in mind?" while scanning the directory open on the desk in front of her, she could have cheerfully curled up and died of embarrassment.

"Well, uh—" she looked at the other faces surrounding her and surreptitiously pointed out Harding's name "—this one here." She blocked the others' view with her free hand.

"Nah, you don't want him. The guy's garbage is loaded with bank overdrafts and lawyers' notices. They're getting him for nonpayment of child support, you know. Oh, yeah, and Lean Cuisine boxes that he's microwaved. The guy has to be 250 pounds, easy.''

"Oh, well, perhaps some other—"

"Nah, you listen to old Uncle Frank. This is your big chance. Now just sit tight while we load the stuff in his car." Frank patted his coveralls pocket importantly. "I've got the big man's keys right here. Then," he said, leaning to stage-whisper conspiratorially, "all you gotta do is look pretty. You'll be sitting right under his nose on that big front seat of his. Piece of cake, I'm tellin' you."

He and his cohorts left to load the big pile of toys into the big rear seat of the big man's big car while Lucia smiled a sick little guilty smile to Roseanne and Tom at their desks nearby. Their pretense of doing any work was quickly dropped as the room cleared.

"What the hell is going on?" Tom demanded immediately. "Who are you going after? I hope it's not who I'm thinking it is."

Lucia looked pained as well as slightly nauseated, while Roseanne intoned dramatically, "The big cheese, the head honcho, the big banana, the head head, the—"

"Oh, please," Lucia moaned as she leaned back in her chair, while closing her eyes and placing fingertips at her temples. "I am simply not up to this."

"He'll eat you up in five minutes and not even stop to spit out the bones," Roseanne contributed uncharitably.

What a perfectly awful mental picture.

Lucia opened her eyes and gave Roseanne a disgusted look. "Thanks a bunch." The older woman shrugged in a not terribly apologetic manner. "None of this was my idea. Mr. Statler just happened to be leaving work while I was finishing up the package wrapping last night, and possibly might have gotten a mistaken view of me."

"How so?"

"Well, there is just the tiniest, barest, most remote possibility he might see me as a man-hungry marriage-minded mama intent on wreaking havoc on the ranks of his poor defenseless unmarrieds," she admitted. "I think this is his defense for keeping the company from running amok."

"So he's going to cloister you off with a personal bodyguard to prevent sabotage from within?"

Lucia squirmed in her chair uncomfortably. "I guess."

"Huh. Frank's right. Go for it. Give him hell."

"Forget it," Lucia said. "I'm sure he's just keeping his staff out of what he sees as harm's way."

Tom came right back. "No, the man's interested or he wouldn't bother. He'd sic some bottom-line manager-type on you who owed him a few."

"Come on, guys. Give me a break."

"Seriously."

Roseanne gathered up a handful of paper clips from their container on her desk and trickled them through her fingers. It was a habit of hers when she was thinking. "How'd he get the idea you were husband-hunting in the first place?"

"Well, uh . . ."

Tom grinned broadly and teased, "She probably said something subtle along the lines of 'Are you married, Mr. Statler, sir? If not, I happen to be available. Of course, if you're already taken, I'm open for referrals should you know of a handsome hunk such as yourself, sir, who might be on the market, sir.'" Tom laughed at his own humor. Lucia certainly didn't. "Can't you just see it?" He chuckled merrily. "She'd be batting those big baby blues of hers and he'd—"

"Can't you make him stop?" Lucia implored Roseanne. Roseanne helplessly shrugged her well-padded shoulders.

"I mean, it's just so funny," Tom continued while Lucia's indignation grew. "You're so cute, and...oh, I don't know...cornfieldy.... And Mr. Suave Sophistication down the hall has you pegged as Mata Hari. Oh, the mental imagery is just too much...." And he was gone off the deep end laughing again.

Lucia was starting to resemble a puffer fish in full puff. Cornfieldy, indeed. So she had a few freckles. Big deal. Who was without their little crosses to bear in this life?

"Uh, listen, Tom," Roseanne interrupted, looking slightly uneasy as he showed no signs of getting himself back under control and Lucia's face became both mottled and flushed. "We've got some things to finish up here before we can leave for the party. We'd better—"

But Tom was having too good a time to heed any warning signals at this point. "I don't know a single guy on the staff here who doesn't think you're as cute as a button. They all see you as their little sister, for crying out loud. You're not going to disrupt the flow around here. Maybe I should talk to the guy, huh? Kind of explain things to him."

That did it. Now she was a button. "All of my life," she announced slowly through clenched teeth as she rose from her desk to lean across it and glare at Tom, "my mother, my father and my brothers have warned me about men and their lines. They're only after one thing, my brothers always said. And I guess they should know. And I ought to always remember, *Why should they buy the cow if they can get the milk for free?* If a man won't take no for an answer, I'm to remind myself that *men are like streetcars. There's always another one coming,* and *drop him like a hot potato.* My father has explained the difference between the kind of girl a man sleeps with and the kind he's willing to marry. Men are also big on not buying secondhand merchandise, and I've been warned of the emptiness of promises to respect one in the morning.''

Tom shrank back in his chair as her agitation increased, finally aware that his humor had crossed some invisible line.

''I have practiced put-downs for pawing males,'' she ranted on, ''from the time I turned fourteen years old. I've got a million of them. One for every possible occasion. They range from the ever-popular 'Unhand me, you cad' to 'What kind of girl do you take me for?' And they go on ad infinitum. Now here's the bad news. I have never, not even once, had the opportunity to use even one!'' Tears sprang into her eyes. ''What's wrong with me? Why doesn't anyone lust after my body? Couldn't somebody, just once, want to play pattycake and not mean a child's hand game? I don't want to be everybody-in-pants's little sister. Whatever happened to good old-fashioned American lust?''

She was out from behind her desk now, openly crying. She needed to get to the bathroom where she could blow her nose and compose herself in private. She made a run for it, but her blurred vision failed to take in the obstacle in the doorway. She ran smack into Daniel Statler, who looked down at her in amazement.

''I quit!'' Lucia shouted up in the direction of his head, before pushing off his taut waist and taking off in the direction of the ladies' room.

''What the devil was that all about?'' The boss's voice boomed into the soundless room as he watched her skirt switch around the bend in the hall.

Tom was too clearly stunned to be anything but totally honest. ''She's upset because she's never been propositioned,'' he said, his surprise readily apparent.

Chapter Two

Lucia huddled in her shoulder-harness safety belt, way over by the passenger door, while Daniel's massive body strained against his own strap. He was fuming. He should never have stopped on his way out the door last night, he castigated himself. Better men than he had been cut down in their prime by little bits of fluff like Lucia. Next time he would keep his eyes straight forward and make a beeline for the nearest exit. Moodily he tapped the steering wheel in a Sousa cadence from his university marching-band days, while staring through the windshield at the light that had dared go red before he'd gotten through the intersection.

The problem was, of course, there was no protocol of which he was aware that would have covered the situation he had walked into last night. He had been a Boy Scout, for God's sake. How could he have walked out and left a woman like Lucia Callahan to struggle through on her own? She had displayed no mechanical aptitude that he could see. She would have been there all night. He glared in her direction as she snuffled and rooted through her oversize handbag, probably in search of a Kleenex. With a resigned sigh, he snapped his own pristine white handkerchief out of his pocket and dangled it from two fingers about an inch from her nose.

Lucia took it and blew. "Thank you." She sniffed.

"You're quite welcome." It sounded insincere.

Just look where his interference has gotten him, Daniel silently ranted on. You only had to look at the woman to know she was as innocent and gullible as they came. Belonged on the Kellogg's Corn Flakes box. Miss Kansas. Better yet, Miss Wisconsin. A dairy farmer's daughter. All that wholesome cheese. Yeah, that was it, Miss Wisconsin.

He gunned the motor impatiently and then immediately took his foot off the accelerator as he spotted the red lights of a car containing a pair of Chicago's finest.

So little Miss Wisconsin wanted to delve into life's mysteries, find a soul mate. Only she was going to apply "logic" to the search. Surely that was a new twist to an inherently illogical subject. If she hadn't zeroed in on his company for her husband raid, it would have been no skin off his nose. In fact, there was a time when he wouldn't have been that averse to helping her down the primrose path himself. But any trail he would travel wouldn't lead to marriage.

Besides, this woman inspired…protectiveness, not lust. Well, forewarned was forearmed. What he ought to do was sic some short wimp on her. Let's see, who was short that he didn't like? There was Field, who was just about a lost cause as an account representative. Nah, not even a fluff head like Lucia deserved him. She would find out too late you couldn't shop for a husband by size like a damn dress or pair of shoes. Geez, she could end up with *anybody*, since she didn't seem to be employing any kind of weeding process other than by height. What if it was somebody with no sense of humor who never thought of anything but work? She would curl up and die. Worse, a guy who couldn't hang on to a job at all?

He was filled with dismay by the masochistic need he felt to protect her. A thankless process, he was sure, that like his mother's childhood spankings would hurt him far more than it would her. It just wasn't . . . him. Besides, how did one go about saving someone's virtue if said someone didn't want to be saved?

Lucia was ignoring him and repairing her smoky eye shadow when he pulled off Lake Shore Drive and onto the little spit of land that kept the planetarium from falling into Lake Michigan. A plane swooped in low on its approach to Meigs Field, the airstrip adjacent to the planetarium, its wings wobbling due to the fierce crosswinds the lake inspired. Lucia ducked instinctively.

"You're gilding the lily, honey," he told her as he guided the car into a loading zone. The fresh-scrubbed wholesome look was starting to grow on him.

"I don't want to look washed out," she said defensively, while defiantly brushing a little rouge on her pale cheeks.

"You look like a twelve-year-old who's gotten into her mother's makeup," he grumbled, opening his door. It wasn't true, but for some reason he objected to her gussying up for even a nameless, faceless "other" man.

Well, Lucia had had it with cute. She swiped quickly at her lips with a cinnamon gloss. "Tough," she muttered before she blotted her lips on his handkerchief and climbed out of the car to shiver in the December wind whipping in off the lake. She noticed *he* didn't shiver. It was probably asking too much to expect him to react normally to the elements.

They used a wooden doorstop they found to hold the outer door open while they unloaded the car and carted assorted doll buggies, boxes of bakery cookies and various other party necessities into the large private room allotted to their gathering.

Daniel watched while Lucia and her cohorts prepared the room for the festivities. Other officers of the club arrived, and Lucia directed traffic while she hung green and red crepe paper streamers. It was utter chaos, pure and simple. There was no discernible plan that Daniel could see. Gifts were stacked in a seemingly haphazard fashion. Red satin ornament balls rolled around the floor. And the food tables kept being rearranged.

Yet at twelve o'clock, when the first employees walked through the doors, everything had fallen into place. The room was festive and bright, the food steaming and ready. And Lucia had disappeared.

Disappeared? Daniel frowned as his concentrated gaze searched the room. Where had she gone? Probably off to tackle some unsuspecting caterer.

He rose from his chair to begin an active search. She must have hired an entertainer as well as a caricature artist, he noticed, and his brow sank farther over his eyes. If she'd gone over budget, he would wring her neck. These damn parties cost the company a fortune as it was. He went right by the bald man churning out cartoons of employees' children. But he did a double take as he passed the elf twisting skinny pastel balloons into poodles for the clamoring little girls and swords with belts for the boys. It couldn't be. A garish red yarn wig covered any trace of the long blond hair that would have identified Lucia. But the height was right. And those blue eyes were unmistakable.

"Lucia?"

"Sir?" She mimicked his questioning tone perfectly.

Daniel looked around him in frustration. He couldn't talk there. He began a determined campaign to edge her away from all the milling children. Eventually he succeeded in pushing her through a set of swinging double metal doors marked Employees Only. "What the hell are you doing?"

Looking around as if to make sure no one would overhear, she whispered confidentially, "I'm making balloon sculptures. Want one? I can do a mean swan hat." And she began stretching a long yellow plastic tube in preparation to do just that.

Disgusted, he pulled the offending balloon from her grip. "Cut it out," he muttered. "I meant, why are you doing this, where did you get the clown outfit, and how did you learn to do that?"

"You meant all that by 'What the hell are you doing?'" Her eyes widened in feigned astonishment, and Daniel was promptly trapped in their depths. "Let me see now." She held up her hand to tick off her fingers. "I am doing this to keep the children entertained until the sky show starts. The clown suit is mine, I made it years ago. And I taught myself to make balloon animals so I could entertain at little kids' birthday parties. I did it all through high school and college. And," she added as though it were significant, "my parents approved."

He quirked an eyebrow in silent inquiry, the brevity of his communications reaching a new peak.

It was amazing how she was beginning to understand his silent communications. "It was the only thing they thought wouldn't be too tiring for a little thing like me," she said wryly. "Obviously, they haven't been to too many three-year-olds' birthday parties."

"They were right to try and protect you, honey."

"I think I've done very well, all things considered," she returned indignantly. "And I could've done the buggies, too."

He tried to soothe her ire by rubbing his hands along her stiff shoulders and arms. "I'm not sure even *I*—" he made it sound as if he were the ruler by which all else was to be measured "—would have the stamina to take on what you've tried to do in the past twenty-four hours. You've got to be running on steam alone at this point."

Disdainfully removing his hands from her body, she retorted succinctly, "Drop dead."

Not the most tactful thing to say to one's boss, and she could see the effort he exerted to control his irritation. "Somebody needs to watch out for you, now that your parents are so far away."

"I'm looking for a partner, not a caretaker," she said with a sniff. "I left Chillicothe to get *away* from people watching over me. And why you care one way or another is beyond me. I'm involved in a logical, well-thought-out procedure to find a husband, and I'm doing it precisely by the book," she informed him loftily.

"You mean there's a book out there that coaches women in man trapping?" He looked appalled at the very idea.

"Hey! It's better than a singles bar."

He cringed at the thought of Lucia let loose in a singles bar.

"All it does is place me in a position of visibility so that some lonely male has the opportunity to see what a great deal he's passing up."

They were passing up a massive migraine, that was what. "Oh, Lord." He sighed and put his forearm on the khaki wall. His head immediately followed.

"He can look, too," she allowed breezily. "But to tell the truth, I can do without any more know-it-alls at the moment. Now if you will excuse me, I am hostessing a party here. It's a little difficult to do from the back hall."

Daniel straightened. "Let's get things straight right from the start. It's *my* company and *my* company's funds. I am the host, you are merely my agent. So, if you want to be acting hostess, you'll have to stick by me."

"Oh, but—"

"No buts about it, my little man-hungry lemon shark." He took her firmly by the elbow and drew her back into the crowded room.

Daniel sent her to change about twenty minutes before the sky show began, firmly turning down any further request for popped poodle balloon replacements. He stayed right at her side with a possessive hand cupped under her elbow as they made their way into the sky theater, and plunked his massive body carelessly into the narrow seat adjacent to hers, effectively blocking any more eligible males from showing interest. Lucia fumed through the entire presentation, not even noticing when the chairs reclined automatically. She simply found herself staring up at the rounded darkened ceiling as pinpoints of lights representing various stars and constellations were projected and moved about on the black dome above.

Lucia poked around the planetarium after the formal presentation was over, hoping to bore Daniel into going home without her. It would be a great excuse to request a ride with Neil Amling. He was short and a manager to boot.

But it was not to be. Daniel wasn't put off in the slightest. As fascinated as she, he gazed at early telescopes and marveled at the accomplishments of the early astronomers. Finally, they had to leave or be late for the black-tie adults-only dinner that was the crowning jewel in the Statler Group's Christmas celebration.

Daniel cut off Lucia's feeble attempt to request a ride from Neil with a freezing look that kept Neil well out of asking range. The man was one of his best managers, for God's sake. He wasn't about to let him get involved with the pint-size whirlwind and have his perspective destroyed while he tried to figure out what had hit him. No, it was definitely his duty to save Neil from losing his mind the way Daniel currently was.

He dropped her directly at her Lincoln Park-area apartment, explaining that she had exactly sixty minutes before his return. No female of his acquaintance could be ready for a formal dance in less than that amount of time. As he stepped into the shower in his own Lake Point Towers apartment, he felt relatively safe that she would be there when he returned.

Lucia knew what he was doing and laughed as she applied the finishing touch of navy-blue mascara to her thick lashes and stepped into her floor-length navy-blue gown. The shoulders got patted into place with fifteen minutes to spare. Had she wanted to, she could have been long gone before his return. But there wasn't much point since they were headed for the same destination, and she didn't like the idea of his glowering at her all evening. She would ditch him later, she assured herself, batting her lashes at her image in the hall mirror she passed on her way to get the rather dramatic, if she did say so herself, velvet-hooded cape that matched her dress. The outfit had turned out well, and if all else failed she could stick a sign on her back where Daniel couldn't see it advertising her virtues. "Such a deal. She cooks like a dream and sews like a pro. Act fast, this one won't last." The whole idea brought a smile to her lips.

It lingered as she checked her lipstick and hair one last time and swept out of the apartment to await her overgrown escort in the more impersonal foyer.

The dance was at the newly renovated downtown Hilton. The place was magnificent and everyone seemed to be having the time of their lives. The Statler Group had evidently done well for itself this past year, because the food came in a never-ending stream of steaming trays held high by formally dressed waiters who were in danger of creating ruts in the plush carpeting from the tables to the kitchens. Thick slabs of rare pork tenderloin, tender tips of asparagus and heart of palm salads appeared. Huge long tables burdened with delicately wrought chocolate baskets and other fancy desserts took the place of the heavily laden hot hors d'oeuvres table complex, a magical transformation while the group was seated for the main course. VCRs, color televisions, even two long weekends in Jamaica were given away in a lengthy series of wonderful door prizes, with the winners all properly effusive and wide-eyed as Daniel stood at the microphone announcing names and handing out the gift certificates.

While he kept his eyes on Lucia from his position at the microphone, she squirmed under the questioning glances of the throng facing her, all clearly wondering what a mere clerk was doing seated at the head table. Their eyes swung between Daniel, Lucia and a female manager at a nearby table who was wearing anything but a pleasant expression and was reputed to have more than a casual interest herself in the boss man, while the black tuxedoed band set up on the stage behind Daniel's massive body.

The romantics in the crowd could have been excused for thinking it a night made in heaven. The room fairly glowed with the many-colored evening gowns. Their rich hues were muted in the subdued lighting and enhanced by the darkness of their escorts' formal wear. A three-tiered champagne fountain flowed, and Christmas goodwill and cheer abounded as starry-eyed couples wound their way around the cavernous room.

As nearly as Lucia could tell, everyone seemed to be having the time of their lives. Everyone but Lucia herself, that was. She was too ill at ease dancing exclusively with the head honcho to lose herself in the magic of the evening. Daniel would park her with some happily married couple while he did a duty dance or two. By the time she had made a few polite comments on the loveliness of the decorations and the crispness of the typical freezing Chicago December weather, and extricated herself from the awkward setup, he would be back, swinging her onto the floor for another interminable slow number. Daniel held her too close when they danced, but every time she tried to put some distance between them, he would press her head back into his rock-hard chest. She couldn't comfortably rest her head on his shoulder, so she spent the time on the dance floor stuffed into his shirtfront and trying to breathe. Talking made a difficult situation worse, so she gave up and danced in silence.

Daniel tried to compensate for the size differential by bending over a bit. All that did was bend Lucia backward at an awkward angle over his arm. She hoped his darn back hurt as much as hers did. It would be nice if it took him a week to recover from this debacle. Every time they swung by any reflective surface, she cringed. They looked ridiculous. And she wondered if anyone at work would talk to her on Monday morning. Several of the women in management were interested in Daniel. She knew that from company scuttlebutt. They would have no way of knowing that Daniel had appointed himself as her guardian angel rather than as a serious suitor; they could make things unpleasant for an underling such as she if they so chose. And even those on her own level might be too much in awe of his interest in her to want to associate much with her in future.

It was a messy situation. Very messy. And it was hurting her back.

The evening stretched interminably on. Much much later, Daniel escorted Lucia home.

He sat moodily in his car after dropping her off, staring into space and tapping the steering wheel in another old collegiate drum cadence. He was freezing, but he couldn't seem even to think about moving until he'd mulled the day over in his mind.

What was Lucia to him? Why did it matter so much that he protect his male staff, all of whom were over twenty-one, from her husband-hunting ways? Was he interested in her himself? Of course not! It was merely fascination with the workings of her mind. He would find the new computing system he had just ordered equally fascinating, he was sure.

He stared sightlessly through the front windshield, fogging it with his breath as he thought about Lucia and not the new computers. How did this afternoon's bubbly clown who made balloon animals for impatient little kids mesh with a cold-blooded man hunter? Daniel thought about marriage in general while his fingers subconsciously beat out the crescendo of the Notre Dame fight song. Was there any chance that there would be fewer divorces if people applied a little reason to the mate-selection process? God knew there was many an intelligent male running around the Statler Group building who could flow-chart the longest and most difficult of programs with impeccable logic and ease, yet whose private lives had so many bugs, the system kept aborting before it ever got up and running.

Absently, he turned on the engine and checked over his shoulder automatically before he pulled out into traffic. The car drove itself home. Lucia had been right on the money. They didn't fit together, and that was a fact. His back was still killing him from the few dances they'd shared. Were he to go into temporary insanity and ask her out a few times, she would have to get shoes with twelve-inch heels. Either that or he could have his legs amputated at the knees. Anything, so that she'd at least reach his chin.

She was too young for him. Ten years was a lot, if you were going to take a rational approach to seeking a life's mate. Adulthood didn't drop down on one's twenty-first birthday like the Holy Spirit's descent on confirmation day. Life was a continuum. One could be in a very different place at twenty-four than at thirty-four. One should watch out for one's marbles when one was contemplating what he was at that moment.

For he was going to see her over the weekend. He shook his head wryly as he pulled into his reserved spot and unfastened his safety belt. Lucia appalled and fascinated him at the same time. She certainly didn't bore him. She was completely different from any woman he had ever known. He should run for the hills. He should take cover under the blankets until the little minigrenade that was Lucia Callahan had singed someone else's hands. All the way up on the elevator, his fingers drummed out John Philip Sousa's "Washington Post" on his pant leg, while he contemplated the turn his life was going to take. Because regardless of the logic or lack thereof in this situation, he was being drawn to Lucia just like a damn moth to the flame.

Chapter Three

Lucia was surprised when the doorbell rang at ten the following morning. She wasn't expecting a soul. Saturday mornings were sacrosanct, and all her friends respected that. They'd quickly learned that to show up before noon was to be put to work assisting in her weekly cooking fit. Now they always waited until later in the day, when they could sample the fruits of her labor without putting themselves into jeopardy.

So who was there? Thinking of the picture she must make as she wiped floury hands on the kitchen towel, she grinned and went through to the front.

She put the chain on the door before opening it a crack to see whom she had buzzed in. If the lumbering coming up the stairs was any indication, she, he or it was big. Maybe one of her brothers had driven up for a visit? No, she doubted they would make a four-hour drive without calling. "Who is it?"

An instantly recognizable bass rumbled up. "It's the plumber! I've come to fix the sink."

Lord, what was Daniel Statler doing here? Lucia closed the door and unlatched the chain before opening it again. She nervously smoothed her hair while he did the last flight of stairs, and succeeded only in smearing flour into the blond mass. "Uh, what a surprise! Won't you come in, Mr. Statler?" She stepped to one side and then moved away from the door completely to allow him entry.

"Daniel," he corrected automatically in his verbal shorthand, while looking grimly down at her. Daniel couldn't help but wonder what he was doing there. She looked twelve years old, and that was being generous. Her old faded jeans were snug fitting, but the huge gray sweatshirt that topped them must have belonged to one of those oversize brothers she talked about. It couldn't be a boyfriend's, since she'd shown a clear prejudice against men of that caliber. And this shirt was definitely of *large* caliber. It hung to her knees and concealed every curve she owned. Her hair was braided and pinned ineffectively up on top of her head. There was white powdery stuff in it and on her nose. Also on the rear of her jeans where she must have wiped her hands. And on her shirtfront. She looked adorable.

"How'd you know my sink leaks?" she asked nervously.

"Lucia, that line's as old as the hills." He shrugged, feeling as ancient as the Appalachians compared to the upstart Rockies as he looked down on her.

"Oh."

He grimaced unwillingly before jumping right in. "I thought we'd go to the zoo. That is, if you're not doing anything else." He looked hopeful, as though he wished her agenda was full.

Lucia looked at him uncertainly. Considering the glower on his face, he was sure to be a barrel of laughs at the zoo. But if he didn't want to go, why ask in the first place? "I love the zoo." His face fell. "But it's too cold today. It's only ten degrees out there."

"We could bundle up," he said, sounding rather insincere.

"I hate being cold almost as much as I hate being hot. Even a person such as yourself must get cold in a subzero windchill." She thought about her brothers. Mmm, maybe not. "What made you want to go to the zoo on a day like today?" She crossed her arms and looked up at him.

He shoved his hand into his pocket and restlessly played with his car keys. "It was the only thing I could think of that you might enjoy," he admitted.

Chicago might be the "second city," but it wasn't exactly backwoods. It abounded with museums, skating rinks, parks, matinee performances of plays, symphonies and professional sports teams and a lot of other things she just couldn't think of on the spur of the moment. If freezing your tootsies at a zoo—one that practically sat out in the lake—on a day when the windchill was probably eighty gazillion below was the only entertainment he could think of, Mr. Statler had a serious problem. Her eyes narrowed as she considered that. The zoo, huh? It couldn't possibly be, could it, that Mr. Daniel Statler, successful founder and progressive president of the Statler Computing Group had fallen into the same trap so many of those tall people she ran into did? He didn't believe that because she had never surpassed a kid's height she had a mentality to match, did he? He couldn't. Yes, he could. She contemplated kicking him in the shins but realized she would only hurt her foot as well as acting exactly as he would expect her to.

"Thanks for the thought," she said insincerely. "But I'm pretty busy today. Some other time, okay?" Like after the spring thaw. May, or better yet June—of the year 2050. "I'd love to invite you to stay, but watching me at my Saturday chores would be ever so boring for you. So if you'll excuse me..." She went to open the door and held it for him.

Daniel studied her through slitted lids. It was unusual for a female of legal age to so casually dismiss him. He knew he was too large and craggy to be classically handsome, but most women enjoyed being part of the sensation he created, the money he had to spend and the power he emanated wherever he went. Absently, he unsnapped his down parka, while he wondered about his masochistic attraction to this midget spitfire. "Actually, it might be kind of interesting to see you do your chores. I'll even help," he added generously, looking around the impeccably clean apartment. What would she do now? he wondered casually. There was no housework to be done that he could see. It had to be a ruse to get rid of him. She would have to apologize, and then he could get on with working her out of his system in an afternoon of activities planned to give him overexposure to her charms, such as they were.

He was wrong. There was no apology or flustered excuse making. Instead, she shrugged and headed back to what he presumed was the kitchen. There Daniel was put to work in a cooking marathon the likes of which he had never seen before. "What the hell is going on in here?" he questioned in disbelief as he took in the simmering pots, cooling cookies and cutting board filled with diced produce. "You're running a soup kitchen from your apartment?"

Lucia looked around the room. She supposed it *did* look a bit like a soup kitchen. She plopped tablespoonfuls of cookie dough onto a baking sheet as she responded, "No, not exactly."

"Then, what, *exactly,* are you doing?"

He was getting better all the time. Not only had he used a subject, predicate and object, but there had been an extra word or two thrown in for good measure. "It's a little side business I run," she explained graciously. "You'll pardon the dig, but Statler doesn't pay its clerical help overgenerously."

Daniel puffed up at the slur and wondered where she got her nerve. "We pay higher than the average, and you get all the same benefits as the administration and sales force."

She soothed his wounded pride. "I know, I know. And that's why I went with Statler. But it still isn't a great deal of money. Certainly not enough to pay the rent on this apartment. I'm by myself, you know. I didn't know anybody to ask to share costs with when I moved to Chicago." Oops, perhaps it was a tactical error to let her lack of a roomate out of the bag.

Daniel looked around him. He hadn't given it much thought. It was a nice little apartment in the Lincoln Park area. It wouldn't be cheap. He wasn't used to considering cost. No roommate, hmm?

Lucia hurried on, pretty sure she knew where his train of thought was heading. "Most of the people around here are single and work at full-time jobs. A lot of them put in more than forty hours a week. They can't be bothered cooking for one. But they don't want to eat out, and they're sick of TV dinners."

She almost wished she hadn't rushed him past the no-roommate thought, as he latched on to the one part of her explanation she had thought to slip by him.

"All busy singles, are they?"

"Well, yes, mostly." There were times when she could kick herself. She had no discretion. Her brothers called it foot-and-mouth disease—open mouth, insert foot. If she'd just been able to keep her mouth shut the night of the doll buggy fiasco, he would never have known about her ulterior motives for taking a job in his firm. It was surely not the most tactful admission she'd ever made, and it had just been compounded.

"And you thought if you cooked all those lonesome, busy, hungry *males* in Lincoln Park a little homemade chicken soup, you could wheedle your itty-bitty way into one of their short, itty-bitty hearts, didn't you?"

"It seems reasonable, yes," she said defensively.

He studied her grimly. "Lady, you shouldn't be out without a leash." He watched as she turned her back and began dicing onions for God-only-knew which pot. "And how do you select the lucky recipients of your beneficence? No one taller than five foot six need apply, food for marriage-minded males only?"

She'd thought his glower over the zoo trip bad. This one was burning a hole right through the back of her sweatshirt. "Oh, I'd go as high as five-eight or -nine for a husband," she clarified. "And I'm even more flexible where my business is concerned." She sniffled as the onions began their familiar irritation. "I told you. I'm just trying to put myself into positions where meeting somebody is at least a possibility. What's so terrible about that? I furnish dinners to anybody who wants them, male *or* female. Height is no factor. I even have a few working parents that I provide for."

"How very democratic of you," he sniped, reaching into the oven for a tray of cookies so that she could continue with her vegetables. They smelled good, he would give her that. "And have you forewarned any of these poor victims as to the real intent of your business, or are you hoping to swoop in for the kill on the unsuspecting slob before he knows what hit him?''

The onions went into a huge pot to be sautéed. All four burners wre going now. Lucia took her spatula and elbowed him out of the way to remove the cookies from the sheet herself. "No point in giving the rooster the chicken count till something's had a chance to hatch. Of course I haven't 'forewarned' them. What's to tell? I have a little side business that goes to augment the rent. If I should happen to meet a few eligible males along the way, well...they could do a lot worse than getting stuck with me, I'll have you know.'' She took the cloth off four pans of perfectly risen bread dough, brushed the tops of the loaves with milk and stuck them in the oven. Lucia looked absently around the tiny kitchen, taking inventory of the baked goods that were beginning to stack up. There was zucchini bread, apple muffins, raisin bran muffins, and homemade granola cereal cooling. Three kinds of cookies were stacked in a corner, and a half dozen cakes cooled on wire racks in the center of the kitchen tables, where they awaited frosting. She nodded in satisfaction before reaching for a two-pound box of lasagna noodles and dumping them into a pot of boiling water.

Daniel had never met anyone like Lucia in his life. Her logic might be totally convoluted, but that didn't keep her from being completely...forthright about it all. She couldn't possibly pull off her quest. She simply wasn't devious enough. Lucia just spelled it out, right up front.

She didn't want to be alone anymore, she wanted a mate and children. Not just anything in pants would do, however. There were specific requirements to be met here. So why in the hell was he so miffed that he didn't measure up—or down, as the case might be? He should be jumping for joy. Ecstatic even. He didn't want to get married. He especially didn't want to marry somebody who was such a long drop down he virtually heard echoes when they spoke.

He was just about to make his excuses and leave, the company be damned, when the knock on the door came. Lucia was up to her elbows mixing cottage cheese, eggs and mozzarella. "Come in," she called, not wanting to drip lasagna goo from the kitchen to the front door. "The door isn't locked, come on through."

Daniel's jaw literally dropped. The door wasn't locked? Come in, come in, whoever you are? By God, the woman needed a keeper. Anybody could be out there. Jack the Ripper, for crying out loud. The open-door policy was fine for the government, but the thought of Lucia using it when he wasn't around to provide protection made him nauseated.

And it was definitely a male voice booming in from the front of the apartment. "Lucia, I surrender," the unseen bozo declared dramatically.

Daniel couldn't believe the panic he felt. Had she found a victim so quickly? Daniel, who'd been about to write her off and leave, planted himself very firmly in the middle of the kitchen floor.

The voice was getting closer. "I'm yours for life if you'll just let me sample whatever it is you've got baking."

Brother, what a stupid opening gambit. Lucia deserved somebody who could at least come up with a decent line. Not that she seemed to be objecting.

"Kevin, you know the rules," Lucia returned imperturbably. "This stuff is for my clients. If I give it away, I'll be short for the people who pay me. I'll lose business. Then you'll have to pay my rent for me, and you wouldn't want that, would you?"

My God, the lady was a professional. Daniel could practically see the fishing line reeling the sucker in. But he really got a jolt when the guy finally hit the kitchen door. This Kevin was by Lucia's definition... perfect. He was five-seven or -eight at the most, with a runner's lean body.

Kevin seemed startled to find Daniel there as well and backed up a step, evidently not willing to crowd Daniel's personal space. "Okay, okay," he said to Lucia. "I said I surrendered. I'll sign up. Anything for a handful of those oatmeal-coconut cookies." He sidled around Daniel. "Uh, who's your friend?" he inquired, pretending not to notice Daniel's glower.

"Oh, Kevin Powell, I'd like you to meet Daniel Statler. Mr. Statler is my boss's boss's boss. He came to take me to the *zoo*." The word *zoo* was said with such ironic inflection that Daniel finally realized his faux pas. Well, that was just too darn bad. Leaving her door unlocked in the middle of a major city like Chicago left him firmly believing it was her appropriate level of activity.

"Now, Kevin," Lucia continued, "you're a health food freak."

Daniel perked up. Did that disqualify him?

"You said so yourself," she went on. "What are you going to do with this kind of stuff?" A flick of her wrist encompassed the countertops stacked with goodies.

"Well..." Kevin rocked on his heels and thought about that for a minute. "There's egg in the zucchini bread, isn't there?"

"Sure. One in the entire loaf."

Kevin chose to ignore that. "And vegetables. Zucchini would certainly count as a vegetable."

"Kevin, you're justifying this the same way I would. There's milk in ice cream, so it must be okay, too, right?"

Daniel watched in amazement as she reeled him in. Even her smile had imperceptibly changed. It was sort of coy and . . . flirty. And once she got him to sign, she'd have the additional advantage of daily contact with him.

"I don't care," Kevin maintained stubbornly. "I was tired of alfalfa sprouts on everything anyway. Just as soon as you're back from the zoo with your boss's boss—" he indicated Daniel with a nod of his head "—we'll take care of things."

That was when Daniel realized he was going to have to work on his scowl. It used to be a lot more effective.

"He's my boss's *boss's* boss." She didn't want Daniel offended. "He owns the place."

"Whatever." Kevin shrugged while covetously eyeing the goodies on the countertop. "When you get back, we'll elope. How's that?"

Lucia sighed dramatically. "It'll be just like last week. Your declarations of undying devotion only last until you get the goods, and then I don't hear from you again until the next baking day. You're fickle," she accused her neighbor.

"You didn't bake apple muffins last week," he informed her self-righteously. "Carrot cake only rates a couple of hours of true love. But apple muffins, especially the kind you've got sitting right over there with streusel topping, why they're worth a lot more."

Daniel's silently scowling rock-of-ages routine was failing him. It was time for action and even a few words in his estimation. He grasped Lucia under her armpits and gently set her on a small spot of vacant countertop, up out of his way. He took four of her precious apple muffins and piled them on a paper plate. He ripped off a length of plastic wrap, laid it over the muffins and headed for the front door, leading Kevin like a puppy after a bone. "Too bad you can't stay, Kevin, but we were just leaving. It's been great."

Lucia's eyes narrowed as she watched in irate silence. The man wore beautifully tailored clothes and kept himself fit and trim. But her mom would say *you can't make a horse out of an ass by trimming his ears*, and no two ways about it, Daniel's behavior left a lot to be desired, and anyway, who did he think he was? Lifting her out of the way as he would a piece of furniture! Just as soon as Kevin was safely out of the line of fire, she would give him a piece of her mind he wouldn't soon forget. To heck with checking as to whether she could spare it or not first.

"Call me when you get back," Kevin instructed from around Daniel's bulk, making Daniel think the man's hunger pains had knocked out all common sense. "We'll discuss signing up for the dinner service, okay?"

Before Lucia could open her mouth, Daniel interfered again. He seemed to enjoy courting disaster. "She's busy all day today," he told the shorter man firmly. "All week, in fact. Much too busy for any new clients, I'm afraid."

Now that the bakery products were safely in hand, Daniel's size and implacable expression seemed to break through to Kevin's conscious levels. "That so? Well, uh . . . say hello to the gorillas for me." He edged his way out the door where Daniel already stood, pointedly waiting to slam it shut after his exit.

"I'm not going to the zoo," Lucia called from the kitchen in a very determined manner.

"Oh, well...whatever. See you later." On the off chance that it wasn't just a standard exit line, Daniel stopped the door in midswing, using his most authoritative voice to intone, "I don't think you understand—"

"No. I do, really I do. I was just ... making conversation. Really." Kevin turned and took off down the hall, clutching his apple muffins to his chest.

Daniel slammed the door, hard, and pivoted back into the living room, looking and feeling ridiculously pleased at having routed the shorter man.

"Now see here, Mr. Statler," Lucia began severely the instant he reentered the kitchen. She was even madder than before, now that she'd gotten a look at his smug expression.

"Daniel," he corrected. If he was to be reamed out, it might as well be on a first-name basis.

"Mr. Statler," she insisted. "You have just cost me a fifty-dollar deposit, not to mention the weekly meal fee he was prepared to pay. He was all set to sign on the dotted line and you—"

"Lucia, you cannot come to a city the size of Chicago and indiscriminately pick up men."

"What!" she gasped. "I've known Kevin since I moved—"

He ignored her, declaring magnanimously, "In the interest of my own peace of mind, *I'll* give you the fifty dollars and sign on for the weekly meal service, all right?"

As if that made it all right!

"What I cannot understand is why you are being allowed to run loose up here. Yuo're a danger to yourself and to anything wearing pants within a ten-mile radius of this apartment. The travails of raising you thus far must have reduced your parents to complete babbling idiots for them to be permitting this."

Lucia's hair was practically standing on end as she screeched back at him, "My parents are not babbling idiots, you spotted toad, and furthermore—" But he wasn't allowing her to finish any of her diatribes.

"Then why isn't anyone here taking care of you?" he demanded as if that were the proof of their idiocy.

"I am twenty-four years old," she informed him. "Not twelve. And it's just this kind of attitude that I was trying to get away from."

"Chronological age is irrelevant. I for one am not looking forward to bearing the news of your demise to your parents. They should have—"

Lucia jumped down from the countertop and threw up her arms in disgust. "They don't need to bother. Look at me. I've only been here for a few months, and I've already picked up more protectors and big-brother substitutes than I know what to do with. I draw them like honey does bees." She'd wandered into the living room by then and plopped morosely down onto the sofa, her chin cupped in her hands while she contemplated that disheartening fact.

"Ah, so we're back to yesterday's outburst in the office. I've got to tell you, most women don't break down and cry when men treat them with respect. They demand it, in fact!" He studied the dejected heap huddled on the sofa, not understanding the workings of her mind even a little bit.

"Most women have a private life where men are interested in something other than her recipe files. You think I don't know I'm short and flat?"

He was gentleman enough to remain silent.

"I've got to take an active hand. Nobody'll look twice otherwise. I'll be alone for the rest of my life."

"There's somebody out there somewhere who'll be interested." He was very much afraid he knew whom, too.

"Anyway," she continued, looking on the verge of tears, "I probably couldn't work up the courage to actually *do* anything with an indecent proposal, or anything. I'd just

like to believe I had a little of that elusive feminine allure
that's required to *get* one, that's all.'' She couldn't believe
she'd actually said that. Her foot-and-mouth disease was
off and running at full speed again. She rose to go back to
the kitchen, determined to say no more. The chili was
probably all stuck to the bottom of the pan by this time.

"So you want an indecent proposal, huh?" He was following her back into the miniscule kitchen where the disparity in their sizes was only magnified.

"Save your breath. I'd at least like the pretense of sin-
cerity."

Daniel watched as chili was unceremoniously scooped
and dumped into storage containers. Lids were forced on
with unnecessary vigor. *"Can't have your cake and eat it
too,"* he said with a shrug.

Lucia looked at him peculiarly. It would be easy, she
thought, to believe that the gods had sent him to harass her
now that her mother was too far away to do the job.

"I might have been able to come up with something
good. Now you'll never know."

Lucia gathered all the chili containers into her arms and
turned to the refrigerator where she impatiently viewed his
lounging bulk. Every time she turned around in the small
work area, he was in the way. "Do you mind?" she questioned. When he moved to one side and politely held the
refrigerator door for her, she snapped in annoyance, "And
don't go stand in front of the sink. I'm going there next."

He watched as Lucia set the big pot in the sink and began running water into it. Unable to contain himself any
longer, he reached over and placed his hands under her
arms in a move that was rapidly becoming a bad habit.
Once he had her back on the countertop, he ignored her
sputtering and inspected her thoroughly, as though
searching for a visible reason for his fascination with her.

While he was considering the answer, an unbelievable desire to kiss her came over him. Hell, *go with the flow*! He would dissect the whys and wherefores later. For now, the urge was undeniable.

It took a few seconds for Lucia to calm down and succumb to the effectiveness of the kiss. Her mother was right, she realized through her haze. Two heads *are* better than one, at least for kissing. Her anger abated, but a new kind of tension curled its way through her body. She'd never actually stuck a finger into an electrical socket, but she could imagine the effect. It would be something sort of like this... only not as strong. There was real electric voltage coursing through every point of contact. She wound her arms around Daniel's neck, and they began to tingle, too. The heat traveled along nerve pathways with strange routes. Routes that crossed and interconnected and led unfailingly to her breasts and way down low to the pit of her stomach. No longer angry at having been placed on the counter like a doll, Lucia pulled his head closer while she leaned farther into him and hungrily participated in the event.

When Daniel slipped his hand between them, Lucia didn't notice anything except the increased voltage.

A core of loneliness that had been deep inside Lucia for as long as she could remember felt filled for the first time. It hadn't been assuaged by concerned family or casual friends. She'd been aware of the hungering emptiness inside her, but not the near-starvation for a soul mate. The intensity of what she and Daniel were sharing shook her to her roots.

Daniel hadn't planned this turn of events, and was certainly unprepared for his reaction to them. He found himself as swept up in the kiss as Lucia was. He lifted her into his arms and walked into the living room to the sofa, slowly, without breaking contact at any time. Daniel considered himself strong, thanks to the vigorous workouts he put his body through. But he barely reached the sofa before his legs gave out, and he sank gratefully into its cushioned depths. He'd never felt this communion with another living soul before. It took his breath away. He slipped his hand into the loose neckline of the oversize sweatshirt Lucia was wearing and gently caressed the delicate lines of her collarbone. He brushed across her skin with surprising gentleness, from shoulder to shoulder and back up her throat.

Lucia was dying. In fact, it wouldn't take much to convince her she'd already passed on and was now in heaven. Where were all the clever sayings and put-downs she'd so diligently practiced all these years? Nary a one came to mind in her moment of need, and she hadn't the slightest interest in honing her powers of recall. She was devastated when he broke contact and cool air tightened the skin where her sweatshirt had fallen off one shoulder.

Thank God. He wasn't leaving, but just replacing his hand with his lips. Her nerve endings multiplied magically when his mouth brushed her throat. Somehow, at some point, he'd slipped his hand under her shirt, and now he began caressing one tightly contracted nipple. Lucia considered passing out but didn't want to miss any of this. This was absolutely *fantastic*.

Daniel was shattered. Aware of the fact he was starting to lose control, he lessened the intensity of his caresses and began easing away from her. Carefully, he pulled her sweatshirt down until it once again hung low on her thighs. He lay there, holding her loosely with his head pillowed in the mass of flour-dusted hair that had slipped from its moorings on the top of her head. It had all kinds of good kitchen smells trapped in it from her long morning in that room, and made a man long for more than casualness in a relationship. If he had previously entertained the possibility that he might be in trouble, now he knew it for a fact. For even as he recognized and admired her technique, he'd been reeled in by it.

Lucia lay frozen, her mind spinning as she tried to make sense of the past twenty minutes. She'd never had any problem limiting her activities to hand-holding and moderate kissing at the door. To be honest, nobody had ever asked for more. But if her mother was right and there was more than one fish out there in the deep blue ocean, she'd just run into her first barracuda after a long line of minnows. She would die rather than ask her about it, though. Certain things were not meant to be shared with one's mother.

She lifted her head slightly and found Daniel studying her through hooded eyes. Barracuda eyes. "Hi," she said.

"Hi, yourself."

"Can we sit up now?"

"I think that could be arranged," Daniel agreed solemnly.

She sat against a corner of the sofa, her knees tucked tightly under her chin, and looked so intently at him that Daniel began to feel like a bug under the gaze of an identifying scientist.

"You are the exact antithesis of everything I've been looking for." She spoke bluntly and matter-of-factly, as though she was trying to reason things through.

Daniel could have accused her of reading too much into too little, but he was basically honest and only nodded his head, agreeing with her analysis in a communication shorthand so short it didn't use words at all.

"I suppose that's what's meant by 'chemistry,'" she mused as she rested her chin on her knees and looked him over intently. "I've certainly never felt anything like it before," she continued, her eyes searching him for the plug he'd used to generate the unusual current.

She'd just told him without words that she'd never felt passion before. He tried not to look too pleased.

"Of course, if I can feel it with one person, I ought to be able to with another, shouldn't I? Somebody a little less didactic," she reasoned, as though Daniel were not in the room sitting right beside her.

Daniel stared at her unable to believe his ears. She was incredible, and he didn't mean it complimentarily. "Just a damn minute, now, Lucia. I would like to insert a little something here."

"Oh, come on, Daniel. You can't seriously expect me to believe that you're any more thrilled with this than I am. We just have to figure out what happened and try to apply the same principles to my search...."

His mouth actually hung open, something that hadn't happened to him since early adolescence. That was when John Bartholomew had pointed out the hole in the science laboratory storage closet that backed onto the girls' locker room.

Daniel was amazed at Lucia's dogged persistence in trying to apply logic to the emotional issue of male-female relationships. He'd never heard such muddled, mixed-up thinking in his life.

"If I could be allowed to get a word in edgewise," he said, interrupting her flow of chatter, "I have something to say." He waited for her silence. "Lucia, I'm considerably older than you."

"See? You're proving my point. We're incompat—"

"If I might continue?" He ruthlessly proceeded. "And I've had considerably more experience. 'Chemistry,' as you call it, doesn't just happen between people at will. It can't be turned on and off with a switch. I know, Lucia. I'm telling you, disparity in height, age, background and anything else you can drum up notwithstanding, what just happened between us is unique. We'd be fools to ignore it."

They would be unique, all right, Lucia mused gloomily as she contemplated going through life with someone so clearly inappropriate for her. "Maybe it was a one-shot deal and won't happen again," she offered brightly.

Daniel looked at her as though he'd expected better and hauled her back over and against him. His lips had barely touched hers when she could feel the current coursing between them again. Damn! Why couldn't things ever work out according to plan?

Chapter Four

Daniel seemed content with making his point, and the rest of the day was spent labeling disposable foil pans and washing and scrubbing mountains of pots. Thank God most of Lucia's clients were either right in her building or close by. The deliveries didn't take long, and Daniel got a chance to take a look at Lucia's books. He didn't even try to be sneaky about it, and Lucia couldn't believe the way he blatantly tallied numbers while peering over her shoulder.

He was impressed. For all her flakiness, she ran a successful side business that added several hundred dollars to her working funds each month. As shaky as he considered the business's raison d'être, there was little doubt she had hit upon a lucrative and innovative way to meet males. Daniel smiled as he thought of some of those males' expressions as they had taken in his bulk beside their diminutive weekly meal ticket. He'd been at his intimidating best when Lucia wasn't looking and the client in question seemed to be within Lucia's narrow parameters for acceptability. And Lucia herself, Lord, the woman had enough energy for ten of her size. It made this inexplicable chemistry between them that much more discouraging. He got tired just watching her. A life of chronic fatigue spread before him.

Finally, around eight o'clock in the evening, he got her to sit down long enough to put a movie on her VCR. She immediately bounded back up to make popcorn. Daniel groaned at the thought of another pot to clean. At long last, she settled beside him, and he noticed she didn't complain when he slouched low into the sofa, put his shoeless feet up on the coffee table and tucked her comfortably under his arm. He put the popcorn bowl on his lap so that she would have to reach across him. Her hand occasionally brushed his and he edged the bowl a little farther away, increasing the chance for contact.

Daniel was dismayed by the latent masochistic tendencies showing up in his personality. First, he was reveling in a touch he couldn't allow himself to follow through on, and now he was actually sitting through a *suspense* movie! God, he hated thrillers. Work was tense enough without coming home to vicarious murder and mayhem. He would take the classic romantic comedies of Cary Grant or Spencer Tracy any time. It was embarrassing to admit, but there you were. Daniel was a wreck by the time the closing credits ran.

Lucia loved the movie. "That was great. Thanks for letting me pick it out. I haven't relaxed like that in forever."

This was her idea of relaxing? Good Lord! Daniel made a determined effort to loosen the muscles in his jaw as Lucia bounced up to push the machine's rewind button. "That was horrible," he said. "Imagine being buried alive under a silo of loose corn and asphyxiating like that." Just the concept made breaking out in hives seem a real possibility.

Lucia gave him a curious look from her position by the television. "He was the bad guy, Daniel," she explained, amazed at his objection. It had never occurred to her that he couldn't take a thriller. She was surprised by the little glimpses into Daniel's personality she was getting. Either she was becoming more adept at reading stone and should try her hand at the Rosetta, or Daniel was loosening up, letting her in, becoming almost, well, *human*.

"I know. And that little boy had to watch his friend being chased by the murderer. His Amish faith forbids him using the friend's gun even though he knows right where it is.... Ugh!" Daniel shivered. "I hate seeing people torn apart like that."

His very wordiness told Lucia how upset he was. "Daniel, people struggle all the time trying to apply the abstract concepts they believe in to their real-life circumstances."

"But that's not entertainment," Daniel quickly interjected. "That's pain. And there's enough of that around without seeking it out as a form of relaxation. I can get depressed by the human condition all by myself. I don't need to pay to get dumped on."

Goodness, she thought. Next time she would pick Doris Day.

She went and sat beside him again, suddenly more comfortable with him now that she knew he wasn't as hard as he looked. "Funny I haven't had any response to the card I put up on the employee bulletin board," she mused. "There must be *somebody* in the company who likes Handel's *Messiah* besides myself."

Uh-oh. Discussing her search for domestic bliss was *not* the way to take Daniel's mind off the movie they had just seen. She made a face at her slip and could almost hear, *Don't scrinch up your face like that, Lucia. It might freeze that way.*

She fought a silent mental battle. Keep out of this, Mom. *Silence is golden,* or isn't that one in your repertoire?

But for some reason, Daniel failed to capitalize on her faux pas. He just looked uncomfortable and actually fidgeted where he sat. It was only a baby fidget, true, but Gibraltar's own fidgeted nonetheless.

"Actually, I've been meaning to speak to you about that card."

Someday she would learn to think before she spoke.

"I'm sure you're very pleased with yourself for coming up with such a clever way to meet a cultured prospective mate."

Here it came.

"But it was dumb."

Lucia winced, knowing there was no way to stem the tide at this point and kicking herself for bringing it up in the first place.

Daniel's eyes glinted like wet quartz left in the sun as he got into the swing of his lecture. "I don't ask for character references from everyone the company hires, you know. Only work references. There could well be a pervert in programmer's clothing in my flock. You had your home phone number on that card, just hanging out in the breeze for anyone to take." Daniel shook his head in despair.

Lucia sat with her hands folded primly in her lap and her head slightly bowed. His words washed over her. She'd sat through enough parental lectures to perfect the technique. Somehow, though, this was worse. Daniel was getting through in ways her parents had never been able to. How odd.

"You don't have to worry, Daniel," she said softly, unaware she'd been using his first name quite freely the past few hours. "I can safely be left to stew in my own juices this time. Nobody's answered it. Nothing can happen."

"Of course nobody answered it. I took it down on my way out of the building that night." She was being deliberately obtuse, he just knew it.

Lucia's head snapped up. So, *here* was her pervert in programmer's clothing. "Somehow I don't picture you as all that interested in choral singing."

His answer was gruff. "My mother loves it. It would make Christmas week for her to be able to go to that concert. I wasn't aware before this there was such a thing as a 'Do-It-Yourself *Messiah*.'"

She was going to the concert she'd looked forward to for months with his mother? Fat chance. She was sure that wasn't what the author of her book had had in mind. "Daniel—"

"Your index card said four tickets. We'll go with my parents," he stated decisively. "I'll reimburse you for the tickets."

"They were free," she responded absently. "One of the downtown banks sponsors the 'Do-It-Yourself *Messiah*' as a promotional event each year." She rallied. "But Daniel, the thing is—"

"You were hoping for a more eligible type. Well, forget it. You're stuck with me, at least for that one night." His frown took on such intensity she hadn't the courage to defy him. It was disheartening to realize what little distance her hard-won independence from her family had taken her now that she was faced with a little newfound adversity.

"Oh, all right. I guess it'll be okay," she capitulated in self-disgust.

Daniel studied her suspiciously. "Damn right," he muttered. "Now, the tickets were for the nineteenth, were they not?"

She nodded. Sure were. It would have been a great way of getting into the Christmas spirit, too.

"That's a Friday night, then. We'll go straight from work, pick up my folks and I'll take you all out to dinner."

Lucia had a sinking feeling she'd lost all control over her life. She wasn't sure she would have the strength to regain it a second time around. Not against Daniel. "Um, okay." She bowed her head in defeat.

Daniel crouched in front of the sofa, tipped up her chin and studied her pale countenance. Damn! He wasn't what she wanted. She wasn't what he wanted. Life could sure be a kick in the rear. "It will all work out," he said with a gentleness she previously would have thought foreign to him. "You'll see." He wished he was as sure of that as he sounded. He kissed her very gently, as though she were fragile and might break. He gathered up his heavy jacket, slipped it on and let her walk him to the door.

Lord, he thought as he made his way out of the apartment building. He was going to a "Do-It-Yourself *Messiah*" concert. Handel would turn over in his grave. Daniel had never done anything but beat on a drum for the collegiate marching band. Well, at least he could keep time. He bravely got into his car humming whatever snatches he could remember from high school's mandatory semester of boys' chorus. There had to be something to it other than the long stream of "Hallelujahs" that he remembered. He would look up the thing and check.

Lucia didn't see Daniel on Sunday. She spent the day looking over her shoulder, but to no avail. She told herself she was grateful. The past few days had put her circuits on overload. She told herself she needed space. Unfortunately, by the time she realized she was going to get that space and could relax, the sun had given up trying to warm the frigid December air and had retired for the day in ignominious defeat. Lucia went to bed not the slightest bit refreshed for the coming week, sure that the weekend had been some kind of cruel joke.

Morning came too early. It was so dark in Lucia's bedroom that she double-checked the clock before shutting off the alarm and rolling out of bed. She stretched, and her body felt as if it had spent the night on a rack instead of on a fairly decent mattress. Habit took her to the window and she wished it hadn't. Heavy dark clouds hung ominously overhead. And those charcoal-gray big fellas overhead meant business. It would probably sleet, with her luck. Probably just as she stepped out the door to catch her bus, too.

Monday was also her day to clean out the refrigerator. She zapped some sloppy joe leftovers in the microwave and ladled the steaming concoction into a huge thermos until it more than threatened to overflow. After wiping up the dribbles, she tucked the mammoth container into her oversize purse and marched out the door. Determination bracketed her mouth and lined her forehead. She would pretend Daniel wasn't even there. The Statler Group was a relatively small company, but it was big enough that a lowly clerk wouldn't be running into the president too terribly often. She told herself she wouldn't give him a passing thought.

That was easier said than done. Especially when even the door you walked through to get to your cubbyhole announced the intended ignoree's name in bold script. Add to that the Statler Computing Group logo on every envelope, sheet of stationery and form she picked up to use that morning, and you had...lack of peace of mind, that's what you had.

Her good intentions foundered badly each time heavy footsteps resounded in the hallway outside of personnel, and by eleven o'clock Roseanne and Tom were casting her funny looks and wondering out loud if she'd contracted ants in her pants or Saint Vitus' dance.

Finally, Roseanne threw down her pencil. "I give up. I can't get anything constructive done with your fidgeting around. What in the world is wrong with you, anyhow?"

Lucia looked up guiltily. "Nothing, nothing at all. What makes you ask?"

"Oh, sure," Roseanne agreed, doubt written heavily across her expressive features. "That's why you haven't sat still more than ten seconds all morning. Didn't you have a good time Friday night? There were an awful lot of jealous faces you missed while your eyes were glued on good old Daniel Statler."

"My eyes weren't glued anywhere and he's not that old," Lucia protested. "Do you think?"

"Old enough to know what to do with the likes of you," Tom teased.

"Yeah," Roseanne went on. "You should have seen Eva Conroy's face while you danced with Statler. Oooh, honey. If looks could kill. She wasn't too thrilled that a lowly clerk had stolen the president of the company away from a high-and-mighty department head such as herself."

Lucia looked alarmed. Eva could make things hard for her around the company if she chose. "Was she dating Dan—Mr. Statler?"

Tom hooted. "Didn't she wish."

Relieved but still concerned, Lucia pressed. "Who else was looking?"

"Why don't you ask who wasn't? It'd be easier. There wasn't a thing there in a skirt that didn't have a tinge of green, I can tell you."

"It must have been the lighting."

"It was you. You and one of Chicago's most eligible bachelors. There. Out on the dance floor. Together."

"Lord!" Lucia shivered. "Even you?" She looked at Roseanne questioningly.

"I'm fat, honey, not dead."

Tom guffawed and Roseanne glared. Tom hadn't displayed much tact lately as far as Lucia was concerned.

"But you told me—"

Roseanne waved her comments away before she could even get them out completely. "And I meant it. He's too hot for sweet little things like us to handle, more's the pity." Tom snorted and Roseanne glared again. "But a woman can dream." Her face took on a beatific look as she contemplated Lord only knew what.

"Well!" Lucia sat back in amazement. This was too much. After years of practicing lines and dreaming of being viewed as something other than a baby sister, she was evidently going to be thrown right into the deep end with the company shark. And no time to get her feet wet first. "Well," she said again.

Tom turned off his electric typewriter with a decisive click and whipped the paper out of the carriage. "I absolutely refuse to sit here another moment and watch you two drool over that man when you could be drooling over me. It shows a distinct lack of taste and manners. Let's eat. That way I can drool, too," he declared philosophically.

It was still twenty minutes early, but they weren't getting anything done anyway. So Roseanne and Lucia clicked off their typewriters as well and tidied up for lunch.

"What is it today?" Tom inquired as he neatened his desk. They had gotten used to Lucia's refrigerator purge on Mondays and no longer brought any food for themselves that day.

"Sloppy joes," she informed him absently as she locked her desk and reached for the thermos.

"Ooh, I love your sloppy joes," Roseanne rhapsodized. There was that about Roseanne. She loved life and everything it had to offer. "And I've got some carrot sticks to add." Even those.

Tom looked pained as he reached for the paper plates and plastic utensils they had bought in honor of purge Mondays. "I'll get some chips and pop out of the machine, and meet you in the lunchroom. Here." He pushed the plates and forks at Roseanne. "You take these while I get the rest of the stuff." He turned to go. "Carrot sticks." There was a real sneer in his voice.

Lucia had the thermos under her arm and Tom was holding the door for the women to precede him when the phone rang. "Damn," Tom muttered. "Who can that be?" Since he had the only free hand, he went back and picked it up while the other two waited, curious. "Personnel, Tom." The interoffice phone required no more formal greeting. While Lucia and Roseanne watched, Tom's eyes snapped up and snagged Lucia's. "Yes, Mr. Statler. She's right here. Just a moment please, and I'll put her on." He covered the phone and said as though she hadn't been able to figure it out for herself, "It's him. Big D. For you." Then he gesticulated with the phone for her to come answer.

Lucia rolled her eyes. "Big D" indeed. Of course, he seemed about as large as Dallas from her perspective. Her compatriots sighed with impatience when she picked up the phone and formally responded, "This is Lucia. How may I help you, Mr. Statler?"

"Oh, brother!" Roseanne stage-whispered. "Can't you do better than that? *How may I help you?*" She rolled her eyes.

Lucia covered her ear with a hand and mouthed the word *quiet*. She couldn't hear a thing. But as she listened, there didn't seem to be anything to hear. Maybe they'd been disconnected. "Sir? I said . . ."

Finally there came a gusty sigh. It rumbled over the wire. "I heard what you said, Lucia. I was hoping we'd come a little further than that."

She'd "a little further" him, all right. "Did you need something?" she prompted. "A file? A personnel form?" She absolutely did *not* want to get into personal rather than personnel business with Tom and Roseanne glued to the doorway. Her question was met with dead silence, and her limited reserve of patience was lost. So let him fire her. "Daniel, is there some point to this phone call or are you just killing time by harassing the hired help?"

At that, Tom and Roseanne went bug-eyed. They exchanged anxious glances. For crying out loud, she was talking to the *president of the company* like that!

Daniel decided right then that getting her back into the bosom of her family would be the easy part. Getting them to *accept* her back would take some doing. It would be "The Ransom of the Red Chief" all over again. O. Henry would sue for copyright infringement. "I called to make an offer for lunch. I fail to see how that could be interpreted as harassment," he responded with what he considered admirable restraint.

Now she was caught between a rock and a hard place. There was no way she could answer without giving things away to her eager audience. Her eyes went from studying her tapping shoe to a quick perusal of the office doorway. Yep, they were still there, still looking horrified. She thought fast. "We were just leaving for lunch, Mr. Statler, sir." Maybe the formal last-name-and-sir combination would repair some of the damage in her friends' estimation. "Perhaps I could get you that information in an hour's time?" She turned her back to the door, hoping it would block some of the sound. "Besides," she hissed, "I brought my lunch. And what would people think?" Especially Eva Conroy.

"A woman in hot pursuit of adult experiences can't worry about her reputation. Come on," he wheedled. "Bring whatever you've got up here. You cooked enough for a small army on Saturday. I'm sure there's enough."

Lucia looked doubtfully at her large thermos. It was big, big enough for herself and two friends. But Daniel, too? She doubted it. And she couldn't leave Roseanne and Tom without a lunch. She could live without it herself, since she'd already had sloppy joes for breakfast. She thought fast. She would really rather not flaunt Daniel's interest in the faces of the female department heads. "Okay. Meet me by the front door in five minutes."

"I can't get away until twelve-fifteen."

"Ten minutes. That's my final offer."

"Twenty-five."

"Going once..."

"Oh, all right. Twenty."

"Fifteen."

"Nobody meets for lunch at five minutes past twelve." Daniel was beginning to enjoy the playful negotiations.

"Take it or leave it." Lucia already had her purse and was stretching the telephone cord to hand the thermos to Tom, tilting her head and nodding in the direction of the cafeteria, indicating they should go and eat without her.

"Done. Fifteen minutes." Daniel hung up and had to grin at her finesse. Thank God he wasn't negotiating a union contract with her. It was pitiful the way she could wind him around her finger. He pushed a button on his desk and spoke. "Frances, I'm going out to lunch. Get hold of Jim Tunstall for me and push back our meeting an hour."

His unflappable secretary was flapped. When Daniel passed her desk he noted her shocked expression. The meeting he'd pushed back wasn't scheduled until one-thirty as it was. He'd never scheduled a two-and-a-half hour lunch before, but if the president of the company couldn't do it, who could? Tongues were already wagging over his behavior at the company dance. This would only add a little fuel to the fire.

Lucia had gone right down to stand outside the front doors in an attempt to *avoid* company gossip. She might as well have saved herself the effort. She had been thoroughly buffeted by the wind and frozen solid in the ten minutes it took Daniel to join her out on the sidewalk. Just as he laid claim to her arm, Eva Conroy exited the deli two doors down with a lunch-sized sack tucked in one hand. Her look as she saw them would have been impossible to duplicate. Sort of a come-hither invitation for Daniel artfully combined with a get-lost-or-else glare for Lucia. Lucia returned a strained smile while Daniel seemed to barely notice Eva, nodding and dropping Lucia's arm to tuck her close to his side instead. Eva gave her one last killing look as she sailed past. Lucia felt sick.

"Where would you like to eat?" Daniel questioned as he steered her down the sidewalk.

"Oh, anywhere. I'm not fussy." It was too nice burrowing against his side to worry about trivialities like destination. It was the first time she'd been warm outside since winter had descended on the city two months ago.

They ended up in the Walnut Room at Marshall Field eating under the Christmas tree. Lucia didn't object in the slightest. She loved the magic of the Christmas season. They ate leisurely, and afterward, even though Lucia objected because she should have been back already and it smacked of favoritism, they went for a walk. Daniel pulled her hat low over her ears and told her he had to be sure she was warm since he liked working off his lunches with a long walk. Then he wrapped her like a mummy in his long neck scarf before declaring her ready to brave the elements. Lucia could scarcely breathe, but that might or might not have been caused by the scarf wound around her neck and chin.

They moved slowly along State Street, wondering at the detail in the animated Christmas window displays. Once, at a particularly crowded but extravagant display featuring a woodland family opening gifts on Christmas morning, Daniel took a set of twin boys from a harried mother and perched them high on his shoulders so that they could see the bunnies operate their train set and open boxes. Lucia beamed as the woman praised her partner, and Daniel grinned down at her a little abashedly. She thought he was dear and was pleased with his playfulness. It was good to know he had it in him.

They left the windows behind. Daniel pulled her in to the warmth of his body and directed her toward the Civic Center where a giant Picasso sculpture presided in rust-colored glory over a plaza filled with ice sculptures. The sun had temporarily struggled through the clouds, and now at midday glinted off the brilliant ice, making the groupings almost painful to view.

"Look at that," Lucia marveled. "Isn't that the most amazing thing you've ever seen?"

"Are you cold?"

"How do you suppose they kept the eight reindeer from melting while they carved Santa and his sleigh?"

"We could stop in one of these little restaurants for hot chocolate if you're chilly."

"Do you suppose they had to carve them outside? They're so big, they must have, don't you think?"

"That coat doesn't look very warm to me," Daniel fretted.

"On the other hand, they're so intricate, if they were done outside, whoever did them would have frozen to death while he worked on them. They must have taken days." Lucia studied the pieces, trying to work out the mechanics in her mind. She looked up in surprise when she felt Daniel pulling her away. "Hey, wait! Where are we going?"

"Inside someplace. You're freezing," he informed her grimly.

"Daniel, don't be ridiculous." How could she possibly be cold? Daniel radiated warmth like a furnace. "I'm not even remotely cold, I promise you."

"Your cheeks are icy," he insisted stubbornly. "You must be cold."

"How do you know?" she questioned as he slid his hands exploringly over the small exposed portion of her face. "You're wearing gloves."

"They're red. Good Lord, Lucia, you don't have to be a genius to figure it out. You're such a little bit of a thing, the wind must cut right through you."

She puffed up in indignation. The fact that it was his presence saving her from her normal freezing wasn't enough to forgive the slur on her size. "There you go with the small jokes again—"

But she was not allowed to finish. Daniel lowered his lips to hers. He lifted her onto the police barricade that protected the sculptures and kissed her in a manner that guaranteed she would never be cold again. When he caressed her back, even through her many layers the sensations he evoked were shattering. "Don't argue, okay?" Daniel said when he finally came up for air. "Let me take care of you. I like it." It was debatable which of them was more surprised by the confession.

Lucia had wondered if the ice sculptors had needed gloves when they sculpted and how they could work such delicate details if they had. But after Daniel's display of gloved versatility, she guessed it wouldn't have been any problem at all.

Chapter Five

Daniel got her back to work an hour late. Lucia's cheeks burned at the expectant, questioning faces greeting her return. Self-consciously, she hung up her coat on the hook behind the door and sat on the swivel chair behind her desk. The only sound in the room was air squooshing out of the chair cushion. She picked up her pencil and tried to look purposeful. It didn't work.

"Well?" Tom prompted from his desk.

Lucia jumped. "Well, nothing." She shrugged helplessly. "We had lunch and walked around for a while. That's it."

"Uh-huh," Roseanne contributed skeptically.

"No, really, that's all that happened. Um . . . how were the sloppy joes?"

Her two office mates took the cue and let the subject drop, but their amusement at the odd match changed to concern as the week progressed. Daniel called her desk or showed up personally every morning just before noon and offered lunch. She would protest. He would insist, bull-dozing over her objections in true large-person style, while Tom and Roseanne watched wordlessly.

Lucia stopped bringing her own food and got tired of smiling apologetically for her long absences, so she began coming in an hour early in the morning. That made her tired. She wasn't a morning person, and getting up at six was the pits. Yawning in front of Daniel wasn't a good idea, either. He decided she was overworked and needed to get away more, so he lengthened the lunches. He took her to the Museum of Science and Industry to see the dis-play of Christmas trees from around the world, and they did a lot of window-shopping up and down Michigan Avenue's "Magnificent Mile." Daniel occasionally talked business with her, directing her to have the department work up policies on smoking, alcoholic beverages during the lunch break and office safety. Lucia tried to tell him she was low person on the totem pole in personnel, but it didn't faze him. She thought he might have been trying to justify the long lunches by throwing in a little business and letting her transmit the orders to Roseanne, who was ac-tually department manager.

Lucia knew he was trying to work her out of his system by overdosing on her company. She wasn't sure if she should be insulted or complimented. But she was darn sure that Roseanne's nose would shortly get out of joint be-cause she was not getting her directives through the proper chain of command. It was irritating that Daniel, Mr. Macho Businessman, could be so totally unperceptive. She was about to tell him just that when he pressed another thorn in her side.

"Tonight's the 'Do-It-Yourself *Messiah*' concert," Daniel reminded her. Once again she was tucked under his arm for a noontime stroll. Today they were on the State

Street mall. Daniel seemed to equate size with health. Since she was lacking in the size department, she guessed he was trying to build her up with old-fashioned daily constitutionals. But she wouldn't be surprised if, come April, he lost patience and stuck her feet into a pot of dirt and tried watering her like you would a spring flower. He didn't seem to notice she had yet to take a sick day off. She would have laughed when he reached down to rearrange her long woolen scarf if it hadn't been such a parental type of gesture. The scarf was already wound twice around her neck. Somehow he managed to pull it up another fraction of an inch around her chin.

"Yes, I know." She'd rather hoped he'd forgotten, but should have known *an elephant never forgets*. Her mother had certainly advised her on the memory capacity of pachyderms often enough.

He continued down the sidewalk, his adjustments to her neckwear complete for the moment. "We'll leave right from work, pick up my parents and go to Ciel Bleu for dinner. We should have plenty of time to get to the concert by eight."

Ciel Bleu? Of course, she'd never actually been there, but everyone had heard of the *très élégant* French restaurant tucked high in the sky on an upper floor of an old-money hotel. The food was supposed to be magnificent, the view of the lake fantastic and the prices well out of her range.

"Daniel, I don't want to go there for dinner. Let's just go out for pizza."

"Whatever for?" Clearly, Daniel was unused to a woman turning down a chance at a fancy, class establishment like Ciel Bleu.

"I don't want to be late."

"I said we'd be there before eight." Daniel's position in his company ensured that not too many people argued with his dicta. It was a never-ending source of amazement to him that one of his lowly clerks, especially one no bigger than a peanut, insisted on starting a debate over every sentence he uttered. She had a David complex, and saw everyone taller than five and a half feet in Goliath's boots.

"Daniel, I don't want to get there right at eight. I want to be there around seven-fifteen. Seating isn't reserved, you know."

"You mean they oversell the place?" Daniel was amazed. "Don't worry, we'll get seats. I promise you that."

Lucia shook her head. "You know, I did a report in fourth grade on a dinosaur you bear an amazing resemblance to. A stegosaurus."

"Oh, yeah? As in large and lumbering?"

"No, as in the major portion of your brains being stored in your rear. How could you guarantee me a seat if they'd oversold the theater? Knock some dear little old lady right out of her chair? Thank God I don't have to witness that! It's just that there are a lot more altos than anything else. If we don't get there early enough, there may not be any seats left in my section. Then I'd have to sit in a mixed section and it's so much harder to sing *against* the people around you than it is to sing *with* them. I haven't sung the *Messiah* in years, and I'm not that sure of the score. Oh, crud! I just thought of something. You and your dad are going to want to sing tenor or bass, aren't you? I hope your mom's not a soprano... I'd like to have *somebody* to sit with. Let's see, we're going to have to split up and meet after the concert. Maybe we can designate a certain pillar or something as the meeting spot.... This is really getting complicated. Please, can't we just go out for a quick pizza?''

To give Daniel credit, he was prepared to be reasonable about it. ''We'll work something out, okay? I wanted it to be a special night out for you. I know going out with my parents wasn't exactly what you had in mind for this evening.''

No, not exactly.

Daniel was busy thinking and talking. He was unaware that he had lengthened and quickened his walk to his natural gait. Lucia broke into a half trot. It was awkward trying to keep pace. ''Listen, Daniel,'' she huffed as they finally approached the office building. They were only fifteen minutes late getting back today, and she looked up at the glass edifice gratefully. ''I would feel ridiculous, stupid and out of place at that restaurant. Oh, would your parents be insulted or something?'' After all, it wasn't her intent to offend anyone. She just wanted to be allowed to live her life as she chose. To find herself a man, a nice short man of reasonable weight, and now a third requirement . . . pizza fancier.

Daniel whirled her through the revolving door. She had to move fast to avoid getting her heels clipped. Darn big people anyway. She stood inside the main foyer of the professional building trying to catch her breath. Before she could even unwind the now suffocating scarf, Daniel was through the doors himself, had her by the elbow and was propelling her toward the elevator banks. Lucia had always thought the young professional women in their tailored suits and nylons with athletic shoes looked ridiculous. This afternoon she could see their point. She was buying a pair of running shoes that weekend.

Impatiently, Daniel punched the call button a second time. The elevator had had the nerve not to show up within a few seconds of his first command. He looked at her while she pulled her gloves off, stuffed them in her cap and pushed the whole kit and caboodle into her purse. She ran her fingers through her hair, to no avail, and struggled with the scarf again. "I just want to show you a good time," he insisted stubbornly. "You shouldn't worry about the seating."

She sighed. "Well, I *do* worry about it, Daniel. It's something I've looked forward to for a very long time."

"It was just another opportunity to meet a prospective sucker. You said so yourself." He glowered darkly.

"One of these days," she muttered under her breath, "I'm going to have him stuffed like Samson, the gorilla we saw in the Field Museum of Natural History." Then louder, "You haven't heard a word I've said since I met you. I don't randomly manufacture opportunities, I merely use the tools I have at hand. I really wanted to go to this concert. And there was no reason why it couldn't be utilized for a dual purpose. But the concert was the important thing. If you don't want to go, all you have to do is say so."

The elevator doors slid open and he stuffed her in, steadying her when her heel caught on the uneven floor. She was getting tired of being stuffed, pushed and propelled. And she was definitely buying those shoes.

"You'd think," Daniel muttered self-righteously, "that with the rent I pay in this building they could at least provide an elevator that landed properly level with the outside floor instead of one that half kills a person by tripping her up." Morosely, he studied her. Now she was fighting with the buttons on her coat. You'd think someone as small as she was would be more...oh, he didn't know...dainty, or something. He'd only seen her in makeup twice, and that was counting the clown makeup at

the company Christmas party. She tripped getting on elevators. They couldn't even walk together comfortably, for
crying out loud. Some corporate wife she would make.

Lucia was not what he required. Not with his position
and the places he wanted to take his company. But more
and more, she was what he needed. Being with her, in-
vesting all this time in working her out of his sytem was,
to be blunt, a bust, pure and simple. She was obnoxious,
irritating and had a chip on her shoulder. Unfortunately,
his enjoyment of her company, their give-and-take was
turning into a craving on his part. "All right," he grunted
less than graciously, "we'll go out for pizza."

Now it was her turn to hem and haw. "Listen, maybe
your parents will be hurt or something. It might be better
if you took them out and met me at the theater. I could
grab a hot dog and try to figure out a way to somehow
hold seats in all the various sections...."

He sighed in exasperation. Typical female. Never happy.
He'd seen a humorous quote in a magazine recently. What
was it? Oh, yeah. *Many men have many minds, but one
woman frequently has more than all of them.* "I said we'd
go for pizza. Make up your mind, woman. My parents
won't be hurt. They're not snobs."

"Well, of course they're not." At least she hoped they
weren't. They might not be too thrilled with their pride and
joy taking up with a small-town girl who'd been practically raised in a diner, however. She flapped her open coat
a bit to cool her cheeks. "I just thought—"

"Why don't you just stop thinking so hard and kiss
me?" He draped her over his arm in the most romantic dip
she'd ever experienced—also the only one—and instructed, "A good one," as he lowered his head. "Good
enough to last until we can get back to this later on this
evening."

It was good, all right. Good verging on fantastic. It was so tender and sweet, and hot at the same time, that they didn't hear the doors swooshing open behind them. When they finally came to, Lucia was very, very grateful that the hallway in front of them was devoid of any witnesses. "Um, Daniel, we're here."

"Where?" He brought his lips back to hers.

"Um, Daniel, the doors are closing."

"Ummm…what? Oh." Quickly, he brought her to her feet and reached for the Open button, missing the way her skirt rode up in the process entirely, much to Lucia's relief.

It was demurely hugging her calves, and Lucia was trying to finger-comb her hair into place by the time Daniel successfully subdued the doors and turned to gallantly usher her out. Her cover-up didn't work. It only served to make her look delightfully mussed. He wasn't brave enough to tell her, so he just grinned as he escorted her down the hall, merely nodding politely when Eva Conroy made passing them in the spacious hallway seem as difficult as squeezing one of those old-fashioned room-size computers into the janitor's small utility closet.

She floated into the personnel department, bestowing a vacant smile on both Tom and Roseanne. "I wish I had Eva Conroy's bust," she announced with absolutely no preamble. "I bet I'd get noticed then." She looked anything but ignored just then, but was somehow surprised when Tom had the nerve to choke and sputter on the malted milk ball he had just popped in his mouth. Lucia looked at him disapprovingly. Honestly, the man was getting completely out of control lately. He tried to look properly contrite, but she knew better.

Roseanne just laughed and said, "Don't worry, honey. You're the one that's got Daniel's eye for the moment.

What time is he picking you up and what are our marching orders of the day?'' His eye for the moment? Why did the sound of that bother her? It wasn't as though she wanted his attention permanently. She looked at Roseanne uncertainly. "Five-thirty. We're going out for pizza. We're supposed to set policy for smoking here in the building as well as on-site."

"Oooh, you make me so mad!"

Lucia recoiled slightly, backing away from the coatrack. She'd known all along these secondhand orders were going to get to Roseanne. Daniel was a pain. First he'd caused her to be on Eva Conroy's blacklist and put up with her rather large repertoire of nasty looks, and now her own supervisor looked as if she'd like to consider Lucia for her next meal. She'd never realized how offensive her mere existence could be. "What's wrong? What did I do?" she demanded as if she didn't know.

"Look at you," Roseanne directed.

Lucia looked. "What? What?" All she saw was her blue silky patterned blouse and cream pleated wool skirt.

"You've gone out to lunch every day this week, and you're still as thin as can be. Now you're going out for pizza! All I have to do is *look* at a slice of pizza, and my hips grow an inch." She patted the tops of her thighs in emphasis.

Oh, great. Now even her eating habits offended. Why didn't she just fling herself into Lake Michigan and be done with it? What with everything that was going on today, if the lake hadn't been frozen stiff as a board for a good half mile out, she just might have done it, too. "Roseanne, I was practically raised in a diner. Food doesn't hold that great a fascination for me. I don't gain that much from eating out because I don't order that much in the first place. Besides," she informed her dismissingly, "Daniel eats all of his and then starts in on mine. That is one large man. I'm very grateful I don't have to pay his grocery bills. I swear, the man could outeat my brothers, and that's going some." She used Daniel's size and appetite to wiggle her way out of a tight spot with Roseanne, but the real truth of the matter was she was noticing his height less and less frequently and being bothered by it hardly at all anymore.

Roseanne looked only partially mollified, but Lucia was not going to go out and turn herself into a blimp just to satisfy the woman. So she turned to her work and kept herself occupied for the next few hours with the new W-4s everyone had to file that year. In fact, she got herself so involved in the new government rules for claiming exemptions that she jumped a good inch or more off the chair when the phone on her desk rang. She fixed it with the evil look she was perfecting from sheer overuse lately before picking it up.

"Hello? I mean, Lucia, Personnel."

She could hear a pen tapping out some marching rhythm on a desk top and knew it was Daniel before he even spoke. "You would think with the payroll I put out around her, I could at least get somebody to answer a telephone properly."

"Yeah, well, you get what you pay for."

"And just what is that supposed to mean?" Daniel questioned darkly over the wire.

"It means we run your payroll down here, and most of it goes to your sales and technical staff. Us peons don't see all that much of it."

There was a lot Daniel would put up with, but slurs on his business integrity did not fall into that category. If this relationship was to go anywhere, the woman was going to have to learn to control her rather acid tongue. Good grief,

where had that thought come from? He was merely protecting his company from a slick husband-hunting mama,
and he would repeat that like a mantra every hour on the
hour until his wayward psyche got the idea. Through lips
that barely moved he informed her, "We've had this discussion before, Lucia. My clerical staff is paid above-
average wages for similar positions in other companies."

"I made more teaching school."

"Yes, well, you have to give up something in pursuit of
happily-ever-after, don't you, Cinderella?"

Lucia hung up on him and Roseanne dropped her head
into her hands. "You can't talk like that to the head of the
company, Lucia. And you certainly can't hang up on him.
I'll be the first to admit I run a loose ship, but you just
can't do that."

Lucia felt terrible for the poor reflection on Roseanne
and madder at Daniel for pushing her into it. "I'm truly
sorry, Roseanne. I don't know what got into me. He just
makes me so darn—"

The telephone rang angrily.

The three of them looked at it as though it were an angry rattler about to strike. "I'm not here," Lucia informed the other two. "I stepped out to the washroom. I
may have gotten ptomaine at lunchtime and went home to
die. I—"

"Oh, stop," Tom directed, taking pity. "I'll answer it."
He picked the phone up. "Tom, Personnel. I'm sorry, Mr.
Statler. She's stepped out for a moment. Uh, yes, sir. I'll
pass along that message. Yes, sir." Tom replaced the re-
ceiver carefully in its cradle and studied it for a moment.
"The man doesn't know his Bible," he finally murmured.

Lucia was nervously chewing her bottom lip. She had
been out of line. Worse, she suspected she wasn't to be allowed the time to work up to an apology on her own. The

expression on Tom's long face said it all. If Daniel had been misquoting the Bible, it was probably the fire-and-brimstone sections. She cleared her throat and clenched her hands together on top of her desk. "Uh, what did he say?"

Tom tilted his head and looked pityingly at her. "He said, and I quote, tell the little lioness to come and beard Daniel in his den." Tom waited for a telling moment before finishing. "Now."

Lucia's eyes squinted in a frown as her thoughts raced behind her creased forehead. "Well, let's see. If he thinks I'm in the bathroom, that would give me—"

Tom dashed her hopes for a few extra minutes. "He didn't fall for that one even a second."

"Oh, well—"

"Listen, kid," Roseanne interrupted. "Just go up and get it over with. If you're going to date someone from the office, particularly a higher-up someone, you're going to have to develop a dual personality. One for office hours and another for after hours. The fact is," she said bluntly, "that wasn't very professional behavior just now. Go tell him you're sorry and then call it a day. It's almost five now. We'll work on the wording for that smoking policy he wants Monday morning."

Lucia just looked at her for a moment. Finally she stood, pushing her swivel chair back as she did so. The force of her gesture carried the chair on its little wheels much farther backward than she'd intended. It rammed into the file drawers lining the wall behind her and knocked a pile of computer cards off the top. They rained down all over the gray-and-navy-tweed carpet.

"Lord, I hope those haven't been punched yet," Roseanne commented. Then she gestured Lucia out of her way.

"Tom and I will get them. You just go. Preferably before some other disaster strikes."

Lucia backed away from the mess. If she made it through this fiasco, she would give up dating anyone from within the company family. Even if it did defeat the purpose of having taken the job in the first place. Lord, Daniel had so occupied her thoughts that she'd completely forgotten about her "husband hunt." Obviously she'd suffered a stroke or some other mind-damaging ailment, for not only hadn't she given the quest a thought—she no longer even *cared* about it!

She squared her shoulders and lifted her chin. Deciding to go down in glory, she announced, "I think after I'm done groveling up there, I might work on him to update our system. This is ridiculous. Every other department here has the latest equipment and we're still using punch cards. He can at least provide us with some decent equipment."

Roseanne, who was down on all fours picking up the shuffled card pile, collapsed in a heap on the floor and just shook her head back and forth while Tom patted her back and said, "Don't worry, she has more sense than that. I think."

Lucia sailed right past the elevator bank. Darn elevators. You couldn't trust them. Never came when you called them and tripped you up when they did, sending you right into the arms of some troublesome behemoth like Daniel. She took the stairs up the one flight to Daniel's floor and marched right past his secretary, a lovely grandmotherly sort who took her rapidly moving fingers off her keyboard only long enough to give Lucia an encouraging smile and wave her in.

Daniel's office was overpowering, just like the man himself. It was strategically placed in a corner of the building that allowed him two floor-to-ceiling glass walls. What could have been a drab cityscape was camouflaged by a jungle. That was the only way Lucia could describe it. Ferns and ivy and...things...hung from lush hanging baskets, while dracaena, ficus and...other things grew vigorously from large pots artfully arranged in a large-scale rock garden.

Sitting in a chair with a cane hooked on its back was an older gentleman, rather slightly built, and although it was difficult to judge while he was seated, he didn't look very tall. More surprising, he had Daniel's thick eyebrows and when he turned to see who was coming in the door, Lucia could see he also had Daniel's unusual eyes. They were paler than Daniel's, but still had that odd blue around the pupil surrounded by an amber ring. This was Daniel's father, without a doubt. When he noticed it was a woman coming into the office, he fished his cane off the back of the chair and struggled to rise.

"Oh, please, don't get up."

"Nonsense, child. A gentleman always rises in the presence of a lady." And he gave his son, still lounging behind his desk, a meaningful glare.

Daniel rose slowly, making a production of coming from behind his desk to offer Lucia a chair. "A lady, yes," he confirmed with an ironic twist to his brow. "But this is more like Mata Hari. I'm afraid she'll shoot me and take my head for a trophy if I turn my back for a second."

The old man chuckled. "Why would you want to turn your back on a little buttercup like this, boy? She's a beauty. Your taste is improving, I must say."

Daniel just rolled his eyes. His father *would* prefer the Miss Wisconsin type.

Lucia breathed a little prayer of thanksgiving. It seemed she was to be spared a chewing out after all. The cavalry had arrived in the form of his parents to save her.

Her relief was premature. "Dad, I wonder if you'd excuse us for just a moment. Lucia and I have a little business to discuss before we eat."

Oh, Lord. Here it came. Lucia ducked her head to hide the embarrassed flush coloring her cheeks and clasped her hands primly in front of her.

"This the one had you by the throat on the phone a while ago, son?" his father inquired. "Never seen you turn quite that shade of purple before." Not speaking in full sentences must run in the family, Lucia noted. Daniel's father seemed to use the same verbal shorthand, dropping subjects and verbs at will.

Daniel merely gave his father a rather grim look that caused him to chuckle. "Give him hell, young lady," the senior Mr. Statler advised. "God knows he gave enough of it to my Millie and me when he was a pup."

"Dad—"

"Sorry, son. With my bad leg and all—" Frank waved at the offending appendage "—can't get around all that well, you know. Just pretend I'm not here. Won't say a word. Promise."

Daniel glared in frustration at his father, close to pointing out his bad leg didn't seem to hinder him much most other times.

"Uh, how did you hurt your leg, sir?" Lucia asked in as blatant a delaying tactic as Daniel had ever seen.

It worked, too. "Got caught between two cars in the train yard," the older man said, looking properly pleased by the look of horror on Lucia's face. "Dangerous work, coupling train cars. Being careful doesn't always cut it." His dad was off and running. Daniel sat back in his chair with a sigh, knowing he would have to wait until the end of the story to get a word in. "Yes, indeed. They push the cars back into one another. Takes a good jolt to get the coupling mechanism in proper alignment, too. Problem is, every now and then, damn things rebound when you're throwing the lock. Take a man's arm off at his waistline if he's not watching. Does it many a time anyway."

"You, uh...you worked in a train yard?" Lucia questioned faintly. Somehow, she had assumed Daniel, in his custom suits and silk ties, had sprung from the bosom of...oh she didn't know...a Winnetka, or maybe a Lake Forest, any one of those posh suburbs north of Chicago filled with lawyers, doctors, financiers and their equally successful progeny.

"Forty years," the man informed her. "Nothing like seeing the country from the cab of a train."

"Dad—"

"Knock on the bathroom door, will you, Dan? Check on your mom."

Lucia was amazed by Daniel's guilty look. He literally jumped from behind his desk and covered the ground to his private bathroom facility in about three giant steps. Lucia didn't know he could move that fast. "Mom? How are you? Are you ready for a ginger ale yet?"

"Gets carsick, you know," Daniel's father informed her.

"Uh, no. No, I didn't know."

"Oh, yes," the older man said, nodding his head sagely. "Hates to travel because of it. Can't even go around the block without getting sicker'n a dog." He sighed expressively. "But these tickets meant a lot. Something she's always wanted to do, so she says. Not that I ever heard her mention it before. But she does love her singing. Sings in the church choir."

"Really?" Lucia was trying to be polite and contribute to the conversation, but Daniel's behavior was so amazing, it was difficult. He was still over at the bathroom door, offering every solicitous panacea known to mankind, ranging from a doctor in person to a cold cloth for the forehead. His mother must really be delicate.

"Yes. Danny worries and hovers over her when we come into the city until she's okay again. You have quite an effect on him, young lady, to make him forget his poor mother like that. Did you see the look of panic on his face when he realized what he'd done?"

"I'm terribly sorry, Mr. Statler. I had no idea—" It was just as hard to complete a sentence with Daniel's father as it was with Daniel himself.

"Of course, you didn't. Just found it interesting, that's all. And call me Frank. Never went in much for formality. Millie!" Frank bellowed, and Lucia fully expected the floor-to-ceiling windows across the room to shatter. "Come on out of there. Food's gettin' cold! Little dinner'll settle your stomach and the young lady with the tickets is here."

It was difficult to hear the delicate, weak voice that floated out from behind the closed door over Daniel's worried questioning and Frank's booming directives. But the drift of the message was that Daniel's mother would be right out. Somehow, it was hard to imagine Daniel springing from a shrinking violet, but the evidence certainly pointed in that direction, and Lucia prepared herself to help a frail floral type from the bathroom and across the room.

But preconceptions are often faulty, and Lucia actually had to grasp the top of Daniel's desk to keep her balance when she got her first glimpse of Daniel's mother. Sheer physical evidence told her where Daniel got his height and breadth, and it wasn't from the paternal side of the family. There was no nice way to say it. His mother was an Amazon, pure and simple. Although Daniel was clearly the taller of the two, she certainly was . . . substantial.

"I'm feeling a little better now, thank goodness," Mrs. Statler said in a breathlessly feminine little voice that sounded almost ridiculous coming from a woman her size.

At least she didn't dress in the ruffles and flounces that were so popular just then, Lucia thought. She wore a nicely tailored navy-blue dress that did its best to hide her large frame, low navy pumps and square navy earrings. A beautiful red-navy-and-gold-patterned silk scarf draped her shoulders to complete the simple ensemble without drawing any more attention than necessary to her size.

Unfortunately, her complexion ruined the effect. At the moment, her face was a sickly pasty white. Lucia was afraid to offer her assistance in getting her across the room. What if she felt faint or something? Thank God Daniel went immediately to his mother's side with a solicitous arm around her shoulders, and Lucia was free to offer assistance with the odds good it would be turned down. "May I help you, Mrs. Statler? Get you anything? I might have an Alka-Seltzer in the bottom of my purse if that would help."

Daniel's mother looked down on the top of Lucia's bound blond hair, and Lucia watched her angle her head to get a better look. Lord, the woman made her own mother look petite.

"Thank you, dear," she responded in her little voice, "but I've recovered enough now that a ginger ale is probably all I need."

Lucia found it interesting to watch Daniel around his mother as he boomed, "I'll get it, Mom."

It wasn't interesting enough to be left alone with the tottering woman and Lucia quickly counteroffered, "No, Daniel. You help your mom over to the sofa by your dad. I'll get the ginger ale." She left his side and headed for the bar, leaving Daniel no choice in the matter.

Good grief. The way he fussed over his mother was actually worse than the way he kept bundling and rebundling Lucia on their noontime walks. There was a small chance—one that warmed her insides a little—that after years of living with a delicate mother, Daniel assumed *all* women needed the kid-glove treatment and had not been demeaning Lucia's size.

It was difficult to imagine, and the more she thought about it, the less she believed it.

Chapter Six

Once Millie Statler was seated and had gotten a few timid sips of ginger ale down, her color improved dramatically and she perked up a bit. Cautiously, Lucia inquired, "Um, have you ever tried taking something for motion sickness before you traveled, Mrs. Statler? I have a friend who can't roll over in bed without getting sick, who swears by the stuff."

"Call her Millie, Lu," Daniel's father directed. "She doesn't stand—" He continued to speak as Daniel jumped all over Lucia, tersely questioning.

"How would you know they can't roll over in bed without getting sick, I'd like to know?"

"—much on formality, either," Frank finished.

"Dad, I'm trying to get some information here." Daniel's face looked thunderous as he turned back to Lucia after chastising his father. "Is this friend male or female?"

"May I have some more ginger ale, please?"

"Just a second, Mom. Lucia, would you—"

"Need to eat, son. Getting late."

"Dad—"

"To answer your question, dear, I didn't realize I was out of my pills until it was time to leave, and I didn't want to hold things up at this end by stopping at the drugstore."

"Mom—"

Lucia was becoming rapidly amused by the way Daniel's parents seemed to totally ignore his attempts at directing the conversation. It was difficult to ignore a mountain, especially one threatening eruption. She wondered how they did it. But, what the heck. *When in Rome...* "Oh, you should have taken the time, Millie. I talked Daniel out of the fancy, slow-service restaurant he was considering. We can do that another time, if it's okay with you. Pizza won't take nearly so long. But it *is* getting—"

"Lucia, I want to know—"

"Oh, no need to order out. As I said to Frank on the way down here, I understand there is no reserve seating, and I do want to be where the acoustics are decent. So I brought a picnic dinner to eat right here. I hope there are no objections? It's fried chicken," Millie offered temptingly.

"Mom—"

Lucia got the feeling she was going to genuinely like Daniel's mother. She was the only one she'd met yet who could stop Daniel in his tracks. "Sounds great. How about if I lay it out since you still look a little under the weather."

"Lucia—"

"I'll take a couple of legs," Daniel's dad directed. "Danny usually grabs them all first. No respect."

"Dad—"

Lucia was busily unpacking the picnic basket Millie Statler had filled. "Oh, this looks good!"

Daniel finally threw up his arms in exasperation, took three giant steps over to Lucia's side and grasped her by the shoulders, turning her to face him. "Read my lips," he instructed. "I want to know—"

"You two engaged or something?" his father asked suspiciously.

"Dad—"

"No."

His mother interceded. "Then I really can't see what business—"

"Mom—"

Finally Lucia took pity. Placing her index finger over his lips, she shushed him. "It was a she. My college roommate, okay? And your mother's right. It really wasn't any of your business." She left her fingertip there for a moment, enjoying the feel and texture of his full lower lip. She couldn't seem to prevent herself from having the finger travel about a bit on the rich contour she found there.

Daniel gave it a small kiss before pulling her finger away. Now was not the time or the place. He felt both relieved and annoyed. "I can't help it," he said in what he probably thought passed as a whisper. His parents would have had to be deaf not to hear, though. "You make me crazy." She did, too. He looked down and saw the teasing glint that lurked in her eyes and all he wanted to do was kiss the living daylights out of her. Too bad his parents were there. Actually, it wasn't too bad. Lucia was simply not cut out for affairs. Kissing would lead to holding, holding to...bigger and better things. And that, my friend, he told himself, would lead to a one-way trip to the altar. Daniel frowned at the thought.

Of course, marriage had its good points. If he concentrated for a while, he was sure he could come up with one or two.

Lucia misinterpreted the scowl on his face. "Uh, Daniel, about this afternoon on the phone. I'm really sorry about those things I said to you...."

Daniel was busy trying to make eye contact, and Lucia was studying the perfectly ordinary round buttons that closed his shirtfront, not cooperating at all. So the two of them missed the significant glance being passed between Millie and Frank Statler.

"Why don't you and Lucia come home next weekend, Danny?" his father offered. "Spend a few days after Christmas with us. Do you good to get away for a while. Give us a chance to get to know Lu here and your ma can fuss over you a little bit. And it's not as though Wisconsin is at the other end of the world, you know."

His mother broke in, clearly relishing the idea of getting her hands back on Daniel even if only for a weekend. "What a wonderful idea. You could come up late Friday. That way you'd have all Saturday and most of Sunday. We could have an early dinner Saturday. In fact—"

"Millie?" Lucia hated to douse Mrs. Statler's plans. Meeting Millie had certainly been an eye-opening experience in more ways than one. Seeing the way the men in Millie's life treated her was making Lucia have second thoughts on the subject of why she'd been coddled since childhood. Maybe it had nothing to do with "big" or "small." She felt she owed the woman something for posing the possibility in her mind. And that was why Lucia felt like a heel when she had to interrupt the stream of possibilities for the weekend between Christmas and New Year's. "Millie, I can't come next weekend."

Daniel's mother looked crestfallen as she absently passed around napkins and paper plates. "Well, maybe another time."

Daniel and his dad both viewed Lucia with distinct disfavor in their eyes as his mother passed around homemade creamy potato salad and fragrant baked beans that still steamed after the long trip from Wisconsin in a widemouth thermos. "Why not?" Daniel questioned starkly. The words fell in the quiet room with the finesse of the first bowling ball Lucia had ever thrown. The one that had gone over two alleys before crashing down into a lane right in the middle of some poor slob's set, probably scaring every strike or spare the man had in him right out the window.

"I have my catering business to think about, Daniel. You know I use most of Saturday to bake for the next week."

"Oh, do you enjoy cooking, Lucia?" His mother looked up from the plate of chicken she was unwrapping.

"It's more than that, Millie," Lucia explained carefully. It was ridiculous to be tiptoeing around this woman's feelings. With size came stature and security. Who was going to tease somebody who could do them serious body damage by just leaning on them? "It's an important second income that I use to make ends meet."

"Oh, for God's sake," Daniel burst out. "Give every damn clerical worker in the place a ten percent raise on Monday morning. You can take a lousy weekend off. Hell, I'll personally give all those poor starving clients of yours a week's restaurant money."

Lucia began handing plastic spoons and forks around. She put Daniel's on a side table next to the only vacant chair rather than hand them directly to him. If she got too near, she was afraid she'd stab him with the plastic fork. "You miss the point, Daniel. My food business is just that.

A business. Just like yours. I have a clientele that depends on me. I provide a needed service."

Daniel threw himself into the chair next to the table where his accoutrements had been piling up. "Baloney. It's just an excuse for you to meet—"

Lucia took a step back, gripping the utensils so tightly in her fist, her knuckles turned white. "No. It's a responsible business that I run in a responsible manner. Meeting people is a nice little side benefit."

Daniel made a rude noise. "Meeting people. Hah! You mean meeting—"

"Tut, tut, tut," Lucia interjected quickly while wondering what in the world his parents were making of all this. She plopped onto the sofa, scooping up the plate his mother had prepared as she went down.

Impatiently, Daniel drummed out "On Down the Line" on the chair's arms. "Take Friday off and cook then."

"I can't." She scooped up a large spoonful of baked beans that smelled like heaven, tomatoes and bacon, and savored it while Daniel glared from across the conversation area. She popped the beans into her mouth and chewed, obviously light-headed from hunger. Even Daniel's glares were looking good to her.

"Why not? I'm the boss. I'm telling you to."

"It wouldn't be fair to Tom and Roseanne," she explained. "After all, you've just given an across-the-board ten percent raise. There're all those computer cards to be processed." She turned to explain to Frank and Millie. "We're the only department in the place with such an outdated system. It causes a lot of extra work, you know."

Millie nodded mutely and looked back at her son. His eyes had all but disappeared as his brows lowered farther at this latest slap.

Lucia sat and tried to look unconcerned with her latest display of foot-in-the-mouth-itis. She took a bite out of the savory chicken breast left behind in the fight for the drumsticks. She could get along quite easily in this family. She hated legs.

Millie was only deterred for a moment. "We'll come back down," she announced from her position on the sofa. "I'll help you. It's been a long time since I've really cut loose in a kitchen. I might even have a recipe or two to contribute to your collection."

Lucia studied Daniel's mother a little uncertainly. Her mother would have something pithy to say about too many cooks ruining the consommé, and it would be easy to interpret Millie's insistence on seeing them as bulldozing of the type she had left Chillicothe to get away from, but even after their short acquaintance, she was inclined to give her the benefit of her doubt. Besides, if the situation got too hot to comfortably handle, she could always get out of the kitchen and leave Millie to it.

"How can you face the prospects of that car trip again so soon?" Lucia asked. "You were pretty sick there for a while. For that matter, how are you going to get home tonight?"

Millie gave a negligent wave with a plastic spoonful of beans. "We won't be in such a hurry. I'll be sure I've got something for motion sickness before we leave. In fact, tonight I think we'll stay with Danny and get an early start in the morning after the drugstores have opened up."

Daniel's face was a picture, and Lucia studied it with interest. He clearly didn't want his parents to stay overnight, but his mother evidently had him wrapped around her rather large little finger, for it was equally clear he wasn't going to object.

"That'll be nice," he finally all but grunted.

Lucia smiled to herself and when Daniel caught her smirk and glared, she put her head down, hiding her grin behind a spoonful of potato salad.

They didn't dally long over dinner, what with both women anxious to be early for the concert and both men willing to go along with their wishes. Lucia didn't miss the glances of condescending male indulgence exchanged, but she chose not to take exception so long as they ate fast between smirks.

Just as soon as she had taken the last bite of her chicken, she rose to begin gathering up empty plates, silverware and napkins, still chewing. As she reached for the cap to screw it back on the empty thermos, Mrs. Statler touched her arm and told her to go freshen her lipstick instead. "The men can sort through things here, dear. They're not helpless. We made the mess, we shouldn't have to clean it up." At Lucia's look of surprise, she told her, "I hate cleaning up after I've spent a lot of time creating a meal. It's so depressing, don't you think?"

Lucia stood there, looking at her, used paper products in one hand, thermos and cap clutched in the other.

Millie Statler shrugged. "I mean, you put in all that effort, and twenty minutes after you put the food on the table there's nothing to show for it but a stack of dirty dishes and a pile of kettles. More work."

Daniel and his father rose at the same time. Daniel took care of the things at his end of the conversation area while Frank cleared Lucia's hands, saying, "Absolutely right. Fully capable of cleaning up a few dirty plates." He grumbled on. "Can't understand why women insist on treating men like a bunch of ninnies who need nursemaid service." Frank thrust a pile of plastic into the waste can by Daniel's massive desk. "Got some mighty fine meals when Millie wasn't worried about the number of pans stacking up, let me tell you. You two run along and do what ever needs doin' to yourselves. Danny-boy and I will have this cleaned up in no time.''

And although Daniel hadn't actually agreed with his father in so many words, he was indeed picking up. In fact, the whole area looked as if it had been policed by a troop of Boy Scouts.

Lucia studied Daniel more closely. He didn't look upset. KP duty didn't seem to faze him at all. She thought of her own father and brothers. They had been most ungracious about helping around the house. Any cooking and cleaning done outside the diner was definitely women's work and beneath the dignity of a high school football hero—or the hero's father. Daniel would have been a natural at football, but he hadn't played. He'd marched in the band instead. That spoke of... sensitivity. Well, that was probably stretching things a bit.

Lucia thought about it while repairing her lipstick in the washroom, while riding the elevator down through the now silent building's interior and while they worked their way slowly through the bone-numbing cold and up State Street to the Chicago Theater. Daniel's father worked his cane like a pro, but the pace was necessarily slower and the temperature necessarily lower with the sun gone than during Lucia and Daniel's noontime expeditions over similar turf. She had never realized just how much she relied on matching Daniel's long-legged stride with her own improvised sort of half jog to keep her blood moving and her body warm. She was half-frozen by the time their destination was reached.

"I'm so glad we walked," Millie commented as she breathed deeply of the numbing night air that came whipping in off the lake. "My head is completely clear now. The air is just so fresh."

Had the woman said fresh? It was fresh enough to bring a tear to Lucia's eye, for sure. Any fresher and she doubted she would survive. Her cheek froze further as the cold-induced tear worked its way down the cheek's thoroughly chilled surface.

"A cab ride after the car trip in would have finished me off, I'm afraid."

Lucia stuck her gloved hands under her armpits and stamped her feet up and down as unobtrusively as possible in a futile effort to restore warmth to her extremities. She mumbled something she thought sounded appropriate and circled around Daniel to use him as a wind block. Mountainous men had to be good for something, and if this worked, she might patent the idea.

They were stuck out in the open in front of the theater until some gracious soul in the warmly lit interior unlocked the doors and allowed them in. It was a few minutes before seven. Surely they would be allowed in soon.

Daniel swung around at her odd behavior, trying to see why she was hiding behind his back. His expression became grim at her huddled, miserable mien, and he began pushing his way through the crowd with little regard for manners or proprieties. Lucia was towed awkwardly behind him. She stumbled and protested his behavior in between apologizing to anyone in the general area. While she concentrated on keeping her balance, she looked around for Daniel's parents. Daniel had the tickets in his breast pocket. His parents wouldn't even be able to get in if they lost them in the crowd, for heaven's sake.

"Excuse me," she said to no one in particular before turning to Daniel. "Would you please stop it? You're making a complete—oh, I'm terribly sorry, sir—spectacle of yourself." She tried to dig her heels in. Frantically, she searched the crowd.

There was a low chuckle on her blind side. "We're right here, Lu. Not to worry. Never seen Danny so protective. About time. Yes, sir. I told his mother just the other day it was time Danny found himself a young lady."

Lucia twisted further. Her arm was going to come out of its socket. God had not designed those particular joints for this kind of motion. There they were, though. Daniel's father wielded his cane like Errol Flynn's sword, cutting a path through the crowd for himself and his wife. Millie grinned and waved from no more than ten feet off starboard.

Lucia just wished they would stop calling him "Danny." Maybe she was particularly sensitive about diminutives, but just look at the way the crowd parted for him, like Moses at the Red Sea. He was a magnificent, respect-inducing Daniel... and she couldn't believe she was feeling protective of him. How he would laugh if he only knew.

She was breathing in short little gasps by then, and did her best to work herself into a snit. Darn all big people anyway, she told herself. When they pulled this macho stuff, people thought it was wonderfully assertive of them, whereas little people just had Napoleon complexes. What she really ought to do was wipe Daniel out of her mind and find someone short, who would have been too cold to have wanted to walk in the first place. Somebody she would stand a fighting chance with. That's what she *ought* to do. The problem was, she'd lost any interest in doing it.

She inadvertently jostled the shoulder of a guy in a suit coat. Lucia was startled to see that although he wore gloves and an eight-foot-long muffler wrapped around his neck, he had no topcoat. "Oh, I'm terribly sorry, I didn't mean—" She shivered against his glare. He didn't seem to appreciate Daniel's maneuvers, and she immediately went on the defensive. Couldn't he see that Daniel was simply attempting to take care of her? A misguided attempt perhaps, but genuine none the less. She was glad when Daniel pulled her on past. It saved her from bopping the guy one and thoroughly embarrassing herself.

They were within a few feet of the doors when a uniformed usher unlocked them and threw them open. Praise the Lord. She wouldn't have to witness Daniel single-handedly knock them in. They were swept with the crowd into a magnificently decorated foyer. This was the theater's first event since it had undergone full-scale refurbishing. It was blessedly warm. And it was just seven o'clock.

She had overheard chatter, in between her shivers out in front, about the beautifully redone ceiling murals. But Daniel whisked them right by the signs for the first floor alto and tenor sections to take them up a graciously curved staircase to the balcony. Lucia tried to pull him back. She was worried about the acoustics up there. But once she saw the seating area, she shut right up. It was...awe-inspiring. Red velvet plush seats. Above them hung a panoply of scenery done mostly in pale blue and gold that took one's breath away. At least Lucia assumed that was why she was breathless. She refused to believe it had anything to do with Daniel's proximity, especially after the way he had made a public spectacle of her out in front of the theater. Then there was the stairs. Stairs normally didn't bother her, but after having been out in the cold so long, her lungs might be frozen or something. Under those circumstances, it was possible stairs might leave you kind of breathless, wasn't it?

They found seats where the line dividing altos from tenors ran right through the middle of the section. Somehow, the foursome worked their way in and were able to sit so that Lucia and Daniel were next to each other, flanked by his parents, and everyone was in the proper voice section. Lucia wasn't happy. She figured Daniel's voice would be so strong, she would never be able to carry her part with him bellowing something different right in her ear, but there was nothing to be done. The auditorium was filling up fast. There was only twenty minutes left before the concert began.

"This book is three-quarters of an inch thick. We'll be here all night."

"It's a musical score, not a book. And you don't have to sing the whole thing. They cut out several parts."

"Hours. We'll be here hours," Daniel groused anyway. "Mark my words."

How could he continue to work on getting her out of his system when they were never alone? he wondered. Their lunchtime meetings were of necessity circumspect. Lucia was so busy with her catering business, Statler Club and the other assorted man-meeting opportunities that she was constantly generating, she would have a heck of a time doing anything about a good prospect should she happen to fall across one. Daniel was inordinately pleased at the thought yet irritated at being stymied himself.

When it came to men, Lucia had trouble seeing past the end of her proverbial nose, and she didn't understand his grousing. "Nobody forced you to be here," she whispered, hoping his parents couldn't hear. Despite his obnoxious attitude, Lucia found herself wishing Daniel *had* decided to come for more personal reasons than simply protecting his investment in his company.

She turned away in frustration. "It's all moot anyway. You're here, and the least you can do is act pleasant about it. I didn't get the impression that you had anyplace better to go."

Daniel was truly insulted by that. Did she really think he would have been sitting home twiddling his thumbs if it weren't for this lousy concert and her free tickets tonight? Why, he could have any woman he wanted. Nothing drew beautiful women like a man with a little excess cash.... That train of thought brought him up short. Lucia was the first woman he'd run into in a long time who wasn't impressed by his success. He had nothing to win her over with other than his personality. And that didn't seem to be racking up too many points in his favor.

His father, who wasn't deaf, leaned over and whispered in Daniel's ear. "You'd better watch your step, Danny. You've got to play a woman as carefully as you would a fish. And this one's a keeper, son. Your mother likes her, too. I can tell."

Daniel contented himself with a meaningful glare at his father. Surely he knew the old maxim about a man chasing a woman until he was caught. Then again, maybe he didn't. After all, this was his first exposure to Lucia. She'd been remarkably circumspect about quoting her mother so far this evening. She was probably coming down with something.

It was eight o'clock. Lucia looked straight ahead, pretending to concentrate as the president of Thalman Home Federal went into the expected spiel on all the cultural events his bank funded throughout the city. She didn't hear a word. She felt Daniel's mother pat her leg and whisper not to worry. Lucia gave her a thin smile. Didn't the woman understand that she wasn't worried about losing Daniel to another woman? She would be happy, downright *ecstatic* to lose the block of granite destroying the cushion springs in the chair next to her. Lucia's mother, who drove her crazy with her clichés for every occasion, had obviously never met anyone like Daniel when she'd informed Lucia time after time that it was *as easy to fall for a rich man as a poor one*. But even she would have to recognize that neither could you *make a silk purse out of a sow's ear*.

Margaret Hillis was introduced as conductor, and Lucia began to fidget in earnest, listening carefully as Miss Hillis went through the score with them, turning back the pages on parts that would not be sung that night. They practiced a few sections. Lucia's face was flushed with pleasure at the end of "And the Glory of the Lord." The acoustics in the theater were wonderful, and enough people in the audience were familiar with the score that, to Lucia's untrained ear, it sounded quite good.

"Oh, this is going to be fun!" She forgot herself and smiled up at Daniel.

Her smile took his breath away. It captivated him. He would do anything for another smile like that directed at him. Climb mountains. Slay dragons. Sing the damn *Messiah*, which, so far, was the biggest challenge of the three. Daniel couldn't read a note of music other than drum cadences. He knew that he was supposed to go up when the notes rose on the staff, but that wasn't quite enough to carry him through the four-, sometimes five-part harmony required to sing Handel's *Messiah*. He contented himself with humming along with the better-known parts of the oratorio and watching Lucia throw herself into the rest of it.

He amazed himself by having a good time. This had started out as protection for the unsuspecting bachelors in his corporation and a treat for his mother, but Lucia was a pleasure to watch. She was so enthusiastic. She had a nice voice, not great, but true and pleasant. She only lost it in some of the more complicated sections that, judging from the facial expressions all around, other people were having difficulty with as well. Since Daniel couldn't *find* it to lose it, he wasn't in a position to criticize.

Lucia's enthusiasm was contagious, and when Miss Hillis accepted her roses at the end of the concert and led the do-it-yourself orchestra and audience in an encore of the "Hallelujah Chorus," Daniel rose to his feet with the rest of the makeshift choir and did his best to follow the guy one row up, who sounded like he knew what he was doing.

Lucia looked as if she'd died and gone to heaven at the end of that one. She sat back in her seat, looking reluctant to leave.

"Wasn't that just the most... It was so..." She fluttered her hands ineffectively.

Daniel made an immediate mental note to take her to more concerts like this one. They seemed to leave her speechless, a condition much to be desired as far as he was concerned.

"I mean, the sound...and...everything..."

He slouched back into his own chair, content to wait out the crowd. His dad did okay with his cane, but why press your luck? So he threw his arms across the back of Lucia's seat and smiled down at her benignly.

She felt as though a slight electrical current was passing through the small airspace between his arm and the nape of her neck.

"Yes, acoustics are a tricky thing," Daniel discoursed as though he were unaware of the tingling caused by his touch. He was very much aware, as he himself was greatly affected, but it wasn't opportune to discuss it in front of his parents. "The amount of absorbent material used to keep sound from echoing around a room needs to vary according to how many people will be present, since bodies absorb a certain amount of sound themselves."

Lucia thought about that while the tingles caused by the presence of his arm worked their way around her body. "But a theater won't always be sold out. The number of people in the audience will change with each concert. What do they do, take some kind of average and work with that?"

Daniel began to play absently with the fine hairs at the nape of Lucia's neck, which did absolutely terrible things to her blood pressure. It was funny, she'd never had problems along those lines before. "No, no. If they did that, the sound would never be just right."

The theater was almost clear of people and Daniel's father rose, stepping out into the aisle and gallantly gesturing the ladies to precede him down the row. As she moved by Daniel to accompany his mother, Lucia asked, "Okay, smarty, I give up. How can you adjust sound absorbance in a place this size to fit the number of people that show up? What if only two people came, huh?"

Daniel looked smugly superior. "They put the stuff in the seat cushions," he informed her with a bit of a flourish in his voice. "That way, for each body that enters the auditorium, that exact amount of acoustical material will get covered up when they sit down. The sound is perfectly adjusted no matter how many or how few people are present. Pretty clever, huh?"

Lucia had to admit it was.

They worked their way down the grand sweep of stairs that led to the first floor. Frank Statler used the rail on one side and his cane on the other and did just fine. Daniel guided one woman on either side, holding each firmly by an elbow as they descended. "Wait here," Daniel instructed when they reached the main lobby. He peered out the double glass doors. "Must be a cab around here somewhere."

"Daniel, let's just walk back to your car," Lucia protested, not liking to have this whole group of large, hardy types stuff themselves into a taxi on her account. "It isn't that far."

"Too far for you," Daniel said. "The windchill out there by this time of night is probably thirty below." And there was to be no argument over his decision, either, for he and his father pushed the doors open against the stiff Lake Michigan breeze and went in quest of a warm cab.

Chapter Seven

Lucia automatically backed away from the blast of freezing air the men let in on their way out. She and Millie retreated into the center of the lobby and began to inspect some of the refurbishings that had previously been blocked from view by the large number of people. Lucia, who hated gilt in any form, found the shiny gold quite effective in this setting. She was just commenting on that fact to Millie when they were approached by a man who obviously lived on the lower end of the prosperity spectrum.

"Hey, lady. The city shelters are all filled up and it's too cold to stay out on a grate tonight. Got a couple of bucks for the Y?"

He wasn't threatening them, although his hands were in his pockets and Lucia had no idea what he might have in there with them. It was more the situation that made her nervous. They were in a deserted lobby, their men out of reach. In all probability, the man was only panhandling. Deciding to play it safe, she opened her purse with the intent of rooting around for a few dollars. She seldom carried much money with her and hoped against hope she could come up with enough change to keep the grizzled veteran of the streets happy.

Lucia was so nervous herself that she didn't even notice Daniel's mother's wan complexion until the older lady had actually begun to sway.

Lucia glanced up in alarm. The man whose whiskered facial growth might have been a five o'clock shadow several weeks back looked equally panicked. He had more cause for alarm than Lucia herself as Millie was listing in his direction.

"Millie, come sit down," she directed, figuring a fall from a shorter distance would be less damaging. Looking out toward the street, she could see that Daniel and his father still had their backs to the theater as they checked down the street for a cab. Men, what good were they? They were never around when you needed them. Lucia was afraid to pull on Millie's arm to direct her to the lobby's available seating. What if she lost her precarious balance and fell before she got her there? "Let's get your head between your knees."

The bum agreed. "Yeah, lady. Sit down. Ain't gonna do nobody no good if you crash." He brought his hands— empty, thank goodness—out of his pockets in an effort to help. In as futile a gesture as Lucia had ever seen, he put them up on Millie to try and brace her.

The fact that the man who had accosted them was now actually touching her seemed to be the final blow that did Millie in. With a low moan, her legs buckled. She used the bum to cushion her fall.

The indigent yelped an octave higher than he'd spoken before. "Get her off me! I can't breathe!"

"Oh, my." Lucia's eyes took over the better part of her face as she gazed at the scene before her. She knelt down and began to ineffectually push against Millie's shoulder, but there was nothing to brace herself against and the woman was two hundred pounds—at least—of dead-weight.

The man trapped beneath Millie was no help, either. All he did was complain on short gasps of breath. He watched Lucia's best effort, a ridiculously insufficient thrust that spoke of the futility of trying to move a weight well over twice your own without a system of pulleys and levers. Lucia panted while the bum groaned. "Get some help, will ya? While I'm still alive to benefit from it."

Just then, Millie began to come around. And since she was no longer quite such a deadweight and Lucia went back to pushing on her shoulder, he was able to work his arms free, prop them against Millie to prevent a second collapse and wriggle his way free.

He scrambled to his feet and took off. Lucia looked up in surprise from where she had been trying to help Millie into a sitting position. "Wait," she called. "What about the money? The room at the Y?"

"Keep it," he rasped back. "I'll take my chances on a grate."

"But you'll be cold." She patted Millie's cheek while she watched the man brush his way past Daniel and his father as they came back in. The headlights of what she hoped was a taxi shone brightly on the other side of the heavy glass doors.

When the twosome caught sight of Lucia and Daniel's mother down on the floor, they thundered over. Frank, handicapped by his cane, still almost beat Daniel to his wife's side.

"What in bloody hell—"

Frank grabbed his wife's hand and patted away furiously. "Millie! Did you faint? I thought you'd recovered."

Small as he was, he was able to prop his wife up into a sitting position. Lucia was impressed. Daniel questioned Lucia fiercely as the two men got the large woman back on her feet and wedged between them. They kept her upright long enough to get her into the back seat of the cab. The tight confines of the taxi brought back the overall skin tingles Daniel seemed to inspire in Lucia. Daniel himself seemed torn between comforting his mother and checking Lucia for possible damages.

Concern flowed and filled the interior of the cab. If the men didn't stop gushing sympathy, they would all need wading boots before long. And Millie was eating it up with a spoon. Lucia was simply amazed.

Daniel directed the cab to stop at the parking garage nearest his office building. He had the attendant bring his car down and gave his dad the keys to the Mercedes. "Take Mom home and get her comfortable," he instructed his father, who was still leaning solicitously over his wife. "I'm going to make sure Lucia gets home safely. Go on to bed. It'll take a while." And he climbed back into the rear of the cab with Lucia, giving her address as he did so.

Why would it take a while? Lucia wondered nervously. Her apartment was on the near north side. It wouldn't take more than fifteen minutes to get there, another fifteen to get back. Did that constitute "a while," or was he allowing extra time? For what?

She sat well over on her own side of the back seat for the short trip home. Daniel didn't seem to notice. Rather, he kept her pinned with his sharp gaze and continued to grill her.

"Why didn't you scream when the guy approached you?"

"He never actually *did* anything, Daniel. It's possible he intended no harm and really just wanted to get in out of the cold for a night," she mumbled. She hated this kind of session. She'd been through enough of them with her own family always wanting to know why she hadn't run to them for protection in this or that circumstance. She'd found it was best to turn a deaf ear. Eventually Daniel would run out of steam, just like her brothers and parents.

"Oh, please. Spare me." He wasn't out yet. "You had no way of knowing what the man's intentions were, one way or the other. Living in a city this size, you can't afford to wait and find out, either."

Quietly, Lucia sighed. She'd learned to keep those sighs quiet. Otherwise, the lecturer assumed the lecturee wasn't taking his pearls of wisdom seriously enough, and then you were *really* in for it. "You're right, Daniel." He probably was, too. "I just didn't see too many options at the time. After all, both you and your father left. That meant your mother and I were on our own. You wouldn't have heard a scream through two sets of heavy glass doors."

Uh-oh. Daniel's brows sank lower at that, leaving his eyes glinting slivers. It was never a good idea to point out the flaws in a person's argument.

His jaw worked for a moment before he spoke. "Okay, I'll accept we shouldn't have left the two of you alone. I can't understand how the jerk got into the lobby in the first place."

"Maybe he had a ticket," Lucia mused.

Daniel looked at her incredulously, as though the workings of her mind were beyond him.

"Well, they were free, you know," she defended.

"Lucia, it was a Handel concert. I don't know too many skid row bums who are into the *Messiah*, do-it-yourself or otherwise."

"How many skid row bums do you know?" she inquired interestedly.

Again, he just looked at her. But the look spoke volumes. "You're missing the point," he began heavily. "And I'm getting sidetracked."

That was probably a first.

"Once my mother had fainted, why didn't you come for help at that point? As you've admitted, we weren't that far away."

Well now, let's see here. Why hadn't she done that? "I wasn't thinking clearly," she finally decided. That ought to shut him up. Men loved it when women admitted to something like that. "That happens sometimes, you know. All that adrenaline racing around in your veins affects your brain. I thought if I could just get the right leverage on her shoulder, I could prop her up."

He looked her carefully up and down where she sat in her corner of the cab. It was clear that anyone her size admitting to such a ridiculous notion as thinking she could budge someone Millie's size with anything less than a block and tackle was more than one bit short of a byte in her brain functions.

But she was right, it *did* shut him up. The rest of the trip was quiet, Daniel having given up on her. Lucia scrunched down in her corner of the seat and rested her eyes, but she could sense whenever a fresh wave of exasperation took Daniel and he would give his head a disparaging shake. In some way, she knew his exasperation was not directed at her, but at the turn of events. He obviously felt he should have been there to protect the "women," and he was lumping someone the size and caliber of his mother right in there with Lucia herself. It made her feel . . . glad. Obviously, size wasn't the deciding factor when it came to inspiring Daniel's protective instincts. Lucia wondered what, exactly, was.

Her relief turned to uneasiness as the silence in the cab grew. And her nervousness increased when, instead of asking the driver to wait, Daniel paid him and sent him off.

"I'll check through the apartment for you before I leave," he explained.

"That really isn't necessary. I'm quite capable of checking it myself."

He draped his arm across her shoulders and tugged her back under his arm. She was becoming almost used to the position. "I'm sure you could check the place over by yourself, Lucia. The question is, what would you do if you actually found someone waiting behind a door?"

Lucia ran through her list of options. "I'd scream," she decided. "Someone in one of the surrounding apartments would have to hear if I did it loud enough."

Daniel directed one of his superior looks in her direction. "You didn't scream tonight," he pointed out.

"That was different," she insisted.

"Oh, yeah? Okay, go ahead and scream."

They began the trek up to her floor.

"A person can't scream just because someone tells them to. The mood has to be right."

"Why not?" Daniel questioned reasonably. "We're in an enclosed stairwell. Nobody's going to hear."

"You just can't, that's all." Defensively, she crossed her arms. "You have to be scared. I think."

"Face it, honey," Daniel said as he paced by her side. "You're not a screamer. Some people are, you aren't. You wouldn't be able to do it."

"Hah!" she said and stopped, puffing, in front of her door. Daniel stood patiently next to her while she went through her purse in search of her keys. When he leaned his elbow against the lintel and propped his head on a hand while sighing in that superior fashion males perfect, she handed him her copies of the *Messiah* score and the gloves she'd been juggling and shook her purse. They were there. She could hear them. She just wished she could find them. Surely his earlier protectiveness indicated at least a slight caring on his part. Losing your keys and acting generally ditzy was not the way she wished to capitalize on it. It would be much better to present herself as a competent, mature woman. It just wasn't likely.

"When was the last time you cleaned that thing out?" he questioned as he took in the myriad papers, receipts, tissues and combs she was rooting through.

"I'll do it, tomorrow, okay?" she promised as she finally pulled out the offending keys. She didn't want to talk about it now, not when Daniel was so close. Kissing close. She wasn't brave enough to close the small gap herself and Daniel only seemed interested in the cargo capacity of her purse. She should have cleaned it out two days ago instead of shopping for the green heels she'd wanted. Wouldn't you know? Her mother was right. She shouldn't have put off 'til tomorrow what she could have done the day before yesterday. Procrastination just didn't pay.

"Okay," he agreed, gently removing the keys from her triumphant hand and turning to unlock the door before he did something rash . . . like hugging the breath right out of her. She was so cute standing there clutching that oversize suitcase she called a purse. But she seemed nervous, probably still shaken by the earlier incident with the bum. Damn! He should have been there. The thought of Lucia being hurt in any way tore at him in ways he didn't like to admit to.

He studied her covertly as they passed through the doorway. She drew such a deep response from him, it was worrisome. Home and hearth were looking better and better. He was having a little trouble breathing, too. The air seemed thick. With what? Love? A gas leak might be preferable. At least you could open the windows and blow that away.

Daniel checked the entire apartment from stem to stern. It was too much for Lucia to hope for that he would quietly leave at that point. In point of fact, he didn't. Rather, he lowered himself into the depths of the plum canvas overstuffed living room sofa that she had reupholstered herself. Her hand rested on the back of a hot-pink-and-plum-paisley chair placed across the room from the sofa. Lucia watched uncertainly as he heaved himself back to his feet after a few moments and paced to the kitchen to fix himself a drink. He came back a few minutes later with ginger ale. She had nothing harder in the house. It was clear he was still highly wired from the theater incident. What else could it be?

He plunked himself back down into the corner of the sofa. The cushion billowed up around him. He motioned her over from where she still stood by the chair. "Come sit by me, Lu. I need to hold you a bit, know you're okay, calm down a little before I leave." He was the moth being drawn to the proverbial flame.

He kicked off his shoes, which didn't reassure Lucia that he was going to indulge in only *a bit* of anything before he left. It looked more as if he was settling in for the duration.

She was a little confused to hear that holding her would comfort him, but it was flattering to think that it might.

She crossed the room, and while she did so he swung his legs up onto the sofa and leaned back against the arm. The sofa was barely long enough to accommodate him. He held out his arm to her when she hesitated. "Come on, Lucia. Take off your shoes and lie down with me for just a minute. I won't bite. Promise."

So she kicked off her heels and clambered up next to him, just like that. Edna's little lamb going peacefully to the slaughter. Wouldn't her mother just die? She looked closely at his face. Interesting. When she'd first met him, he'd been almost homely. Tonight he was almost handsome. How had he managed that? Or was it her perception of him that had changed?

Daniel grunted and cupped both her elbows, lifting her over him and nestling her between his big body and the sofa back. "Bony little thing, aren't you?" he commented. But before she could bristle and think of any kind of comeback, he sighed in contentment, wrapped his arms around her and lost a massive hand in her long blond tresses. "Ah, that feels good. You feel good. My blood pressure's dropping already. You know," he continued, "when I was just a little kid, my parents gave me this huge stuffed teddy bear. It had a vest and necktie and a music box in its back. I slept with that thing for years. Proportionately, you fit about the same as that bear did back then. Haven't thought about him in years." Daniel lapsed into thoughtful silence, still absently stroking her hair.

Lucia put her head back and tried to look at him, but she was too close to focus well. A teddy bear? Vest and necktie? Music box in her back? This man's idea of whispering sweet nothings needed polishing.

However, there was no denying the tiny chills that began where his hand absently massaged her scalp and streaked in little shivers down her neck and back. In fact, every point of contact down the entire length of their bodies screamed at her. She'd brooded the entire trip home over his intentions, but he seemed content to lie there reminiscing about his childhood. She had no way of knowing the struggle going on within Daniel. How he couldn't bring himself to leave, yet didn't want to disillusion or compromise her, either. To her, he seemed to be acting almost brotherly, and she already had three of those.

She wanted Daniel to notice *her*. What the heck, he might not have all the qualifications on her list—actually, he didn't have any—but she was flexible and it was *a woman's prerogative to change her mind*. She was open to a little friendly persuasion on Daniel's part. He just didn't seem terribly interested in applying any.

"The Christmas I got that bear, there was so much snow, my dad pulled me on a sled to midnight services. The snow had drifted and the perfectly flat, square streets of the south side of Chicago were beautiful. All soft, and gently curving hills."

Maybe if she had a few gentle curves of her own, Daniel's interest might be sparked. "Daniel, what would you think if I had a little something extra surgically implanted on top here?" She cringed. How could she have blurted out something like that?

Daniel looked down in amazement at her head on his shoulder. He'd been in the middle of sharing some of his childhood Christmases with her. Memories no doubt sparked by the small tree that stood with its crooked trunk and pinpoint Italian lights in a corner of the room. He was making an effort to get to know her on planes other than physical, to see if there might be something there to build on. What plane was she on? "Lucia, I thought we were talking about Christmas. What in the world are *you* talking about?''

Oh, well. *In for a nickel, in for a dime.* "It bothers you that I'm flat." She stated it as a fact, sure now she was on the right track. Why else would he still be treating her like a kid sister?

"You're not flat," he contradicted.

"As a pancake," she said darkly. "I'd bet my last dime that's why I can't get anybody interested."

"You're not trying to interest just *anybody*, Lucia. You don't want some guy who's only interested in your cup size." The whole idea of anyone looking at her that way made him burn. "And you're not flat. Just...petite. A girl your size would look ridiculous with huge breasts."

See? He'd called her a girl. Not a woman, a girl. It proved her point. "I said I just wanted to add a *little* something."

"Lucia," Daniel groaned. "Why don't you give yourself a little credit? Haven't you ever stopped to think that maybe you're not constantly having to defend your virtue because men instinctively know you're the marrying kind and not the fooling-around kind?" It would be a crime for Lucia to ever be made to feel shame. She'd been raised so protectively. Unfortunately, there must be a touch of the criminal in him, for he wanted to fool around with her more right now than he wanted to breathe.

He sounded irritated. A fully grown, hot-blooded man like Daniel probably didn't buy into that instinctively respectful theory, she thought, and was probably mad at being put on the spot. He just didn't want her. After all, he had her reclining right next to him on the sofa and what was he doing? Talking about teddy bears!

Life was the pits. She'd finally warmed to the idea of Daniel being the man in her life, and he wasn't interested in reciprocating. Just once before middle-aged spread took over she would like to have a discussion with her mother on a need-to-know basis concerning a man's one-track mind and the inadvisability of casting pearls before swine. Just once.

While she was off in her own world, things were getting interesting back home on the couch. Daniel was unbuttoning her blouse! Hastily, she grabbed the two edges and held them together while giving him a speaking look. "Buying my dinner does *not* entitle you to a free dessert, Daniel. I am not that kind of woman." Not bad. Not bad at all.

Daniel looked at her in astonishment. "Lucia, I didn't buy your dinner tonight. My mother brought it, remember? We ate up in my office." He prompted her memory, taken aback by her change in mood. "I was getting the impression that you *wanted* me to be interested."

"Oh, so you're not interested for yourself, huh? This was just a corporal work of mercy and I should be grateful?" Darn him for spoiling everything. If she hadn't been so ticked off, she would probably have started crying. Something was definitely wrong when a man unbuttoned your blouse as a favor to you.

"I never said that!" Daniel roared, losing his patience entirely. "I only meant that I thought I had your approval for what was happening. You weren't shy with all that talk about breast size right out of the blue. I have certainly never expected a woman to put out simply because I might have paid for a meal!"

He was insulted and it showed, but Lucia took heart in the fact that he had referred to her, albeit obliquely, as a woman and not a girl.

"Oh, don't do me any favors." She sniffed, turning her head.

"For crying out loud!" Daniel muttered along with a lot of other stuff Lucia couldn't catch. He'd thought he was tense earlier. This little lady could tie him up in more knots than a twenty-point Christmas bow.

Lucia struggled to get hold of herself and was genuinely ashamed. "I'm sorry, Daniel," she admitted. During all those wonderful fantasies of hers, she'd never given a thought to what happened to the man once he'd taken a little encouragement only to be shot down by one of her fabulous one-liners. "Stay a little while longer. I want to hear about the Christmas you got the bear. After you fell asleep at the midnight service and your parents pinched you to keep you awake, were your presents waiting under the tree when you got home? Or did you have to wait until the next morning to get your gifts?"

But Daniel was no longer really interested in relating childhood experiences. What with her blouse hanging partially open and the way she was lying half on top of him, his attention had wandered. "Well, let's see." He slid his hand down her neck and under the loosened blouse to her shoulder. Lord, she was delicately boned. So fragile. And her skin had the translucent quality of the milk glass collection his mother displayed in the dining room back home.

"Besides the bear, I think there was..." He brushed the top swell of her satiny breast with his fingertips. It was indeed small, but perfectly proportioned to the rest of her petite frame. He could feel a slight tremble take her at the contact and was disturbed by his own answering shiver. Oh, God. He should not be doing this with respectable, marriageable Lucia, but he couldn't bring himself to stop just yet, either.

She wasn't withdrawing from his touch. It would be so much easier if she would at least act mildly aloof and un-approachable.

"I...there was a baseball mitt." There was a slight up-turn in his voice, as though he wasn't too sure of his facts. "And, uh..."

Slowly, carefully, he eased his hand downward. He didn't want to startle her or appear to be grabbing. He eased it over the small lace-covered mound and heard her breath catch, so he just rested it there, letting her get ac-customed to this more personal touch.

Lucia was amazed by the feelings sparking through her. And talk about your instinctive feelings, she simply *knew* that Daniel was the catalyst. She'd been on the receiving end of a few good-night kisses and had brushed against men casually while working at close quarters in the office. There'd been...nothing. No, it was definitely Daniel. But what to do about it? This felt so good, so right. She eased a little bit onto her back so Daniel could have freer access. She hoped he didn't notice and think her brazen or any-thing.

But, of course Daniel *did* notice, and he inched closer to the edge of the sofa so that Lucia would fall back a frac-tion farther. He moved just his thumb, lightly grazing the crest of her breast as an experiment.

She didn't move away. In fact, her back arched a bit as though she were trying to catch his elusive touch. That was encouraging. He could probably bring his other hand into play now.

Lucia didn't want to appear too blatant, but it was dif-ficult to maintain a train of thought under the circum-stances. "So, uh, what else did you get besides the um, the ummm, the mitt?" She was proud of herself for remem-bering that.

Daniel continued to move his thumb lazily across the peak of her breast, just a little more firmly than before. He'd finished unbuttoning her blouse with his other hand and pushed it out of the way, an action that allowed him to rub her midriff and tease the underswell of the other breast. He turned a bit on his side and began marauding the pearly confines of her ear with his kisses. She shivered as his warm breath blew there and he said, "Ginger."

"You, uh, you got ginger for Christmas along with a baseball mitt?" How odd.

He slid his mouth down her throat, encouraged by her lack of resistance, and began working his way across her collarbone. "No. You smell like ginger. I've never smelled perfume like it before. It's unbelievably sexy."

Lucia jumped as he planted kisses all over the upper swell of both breasts. "I'm glad you like it," she whispered breathlessly, incapable of speaking any other way. "But it's just happenstance that I smell that way. You have to refrigerate gingerbread dough for a few...hours before you can...roll it out." She wriggled a little closer to his touch. "So I made the dough this morning before I went to work. I could, uh, I could bake some for you if you wanted...." The offer was tentatively made and she prayed that he turned it down. She really didn't want to put a stop to all these new sensations she was feeling. Not yet. Please, please, please, say no.

Daniel didn't want to stop, either. Through the lacy barrier of her bra he could see—and feel—how her breasts had swollen beneath his tender touch. The nipples were pointed and hard, begging to be caressed. It would take a better man than he...

He looked back at her face. So lovely. So eager to taste life. Well by God, the road to hell might be paved with good intentions, but they damn well wouldn't be his. Lucia needed protecting, regardless of her own thoughts on the matter. Hadn't he just got done telling her she deserved respect and marriage? He should take his own words to heart. He was going to call her parents. Maybe her brothers could— No, that would be the coward's way out. He would take care of this himself. Regretfully, he gave the pouting tip of her breast one last pass with his thumb and felt her shiver again. Feeling more noble than a knight in Arthur's court, he pulled her shirtfront together and did up every button, including the one right under her chin.

He flopped onto his back, releasing her completely, and what with his teeth gritted so tightly, and Lucia not quite out of her sensual fog, she almost missed the tersely bitten, "I would love a gingerbread cookie, Lu. I haven't had one in years."

Well. How about that? Her mother had always said the way to a man's heart was through his stomach, but this was ridiculous. Tonight she'd been prepared to accept that a better way to hold a man... to hold Daniel, was in her arms. Wrong again.

Lucia took one look at the clouds lowering over his brow and backed away a bit. Of course, she didn't know much about this kind of thing, but she was pretty sure the man wasn't supposed to look on the verge of committing mayhem after a session on the sofa.

She sat up, looking at him a little uncertainly and increasing the distance between them as unobtrusively as possible. "Uh, sure, Daniel. I can roll some out right now. No problem." She brushed a few long blond wisps off her forehead and wondered how she was going to get off the sofa without crawling directly over him. In his present mood, that didn't seem too hot an idea. Maybe she could go over the sofa back?

She prepared to do just that when Daniel grabbed her firmly on both sides of her waist and lifted her, with no effort at all, right over his supine body. "Got any raisins?" he asked grimly.

Her hesitant smile faded. "Uh, sure. I'm sure I do. I'll just go and get them. They're right in the refrigerator door. We can use them for buttons on the gingerbread men's coats, okay?"

Chapter Eight

And that was how Daniel and Lucia began baking and decorating Christmas cookies at midnight that Friday night. Daniel, whose end of the deal at home had been cleaning up after his mother had created a meal, began to suspect his mother of keeping the better end of the bargain for herself. It certainly came in second to necking with Lucia on the sofa, but since that was out of the question, this wasn't bad at all. Lucia showed him how to use a garlic press to make hair out of dough and they turned half the ginger men into ginger ladies. Daniel followed a recipe on the back of the powdered sugar bag and made frosting. Splitting it up into lots of little bowls, he went nuts with the food coloring. Once the cookies were baked, he learned how to pipe frosting, and they clothed the freshly baked little people in all manner of outfits. They stuck on raisins and every other type of edible spangle Lucia had in her kitchen.

The kitchen was totaled when Daniel reached for the last batch.

"No. Leave those plain," Lucia instructed.

"How come?" Daniel asked, puzzled. "There's enough frosting left." He sounded disappointed, as though the five dozen he'd already decorated didn't count.

"Those are for the Marlins," Lucia explained. "Mrs. Marlin doesn't have time to do any baking with her five-year-old. I'm hoping she can at least squeeze in the time to decorate a few with him."

Daniel watched as Lucia put the plug down in the sink drain, squirted a healthy amount of liquid detergent in and turned on the water. He began gathering up the empty bowls and utensils to stack in the sink. "You sound disapproving."

She took the pile from him and set them in the sink. "Do I?" She shut off the water and swished a dishcloth through the suds. "I don't mean to. I mean, it's not really any of my affair, is it?" She never realized how tight the kitchen was. Daniel was well within the three-foot halo she was under strict motherly injunction to allow no man to violate and she was hyperventilating. There was no place to move in the cramped cooking area to get a little room and compose herself.

"No, it isn't. But you obviously have feelings on the subject. I'd be interested in hearing how a modern woman who uses every twentieth-century weapon at her disposal to gain her ends can possibly object to a fellow female carving a niche in the working world. I thought that was the ideal nowadays."

"Oh, I don't object to a woman working," Lucia assured him. "Circumstances or personality can dictate..." She foundered, wondering what Daniel was after, and oddly enough, wanting to give it to him. She couldn't

marshal her thoughts enough to present a lucid argument
one way or the other in this tiny, tight room with Daniel
breathing down her neck. All she could think of was his
wonderful proximity back on the sofa.

"But you *do* object to this Marlin woman's working."

"Well, yes. But that's only because she's so...so..."

"So?"

"Intense." Yes, that was it. Intense. "She's totally ded-
icated to being liberated."

Daniel looked puzzled. "Explain." He was curious as to
Lucia's feeling on this score. Was she basically an old-
fashioned girl in search of a man to start a family with? He
just wondered if her feet were firmly planted on the ground
in her search for hearth and home. Lucia was young and
had a romantic streak a mile wide. The daily push-and-pull
interactions and compromises necessary for a marriage to
work would devastate someone whose rose-colored glasses
were too thick. Their age difference was large. He would
like some assurance it was mostly chronological.

"It was warm when I first came here. September, but
still beach weather." As warm as it was just then in the
kitchen. Daniel radiated heat like the late summer sun had.
Her skin was flushed and rosy now, too, just as it had been
on the sand by the lake. She smiled her pleasure lazily
while rinsing the cookie sheet she'd washed. She set it on
the rack next to the sink and reached for another.

Daniel scraped loose and nibbled a final bit of dough
from the bottom of a bowl before consigning it to the
soapsuds. He tried to imagine surviving a life of non se-
quiturs. "Lucia, how did we get onto going to the beach?
I could have sworn we were talking about Mrs. Marlin not
taking time to bake cookies."

"Hmm? Oh, yes, we were. Well, anyway, there was this
couple there. I sat next to them. They actually used a

wristwatch with a buzzer on it to time half-hour periods, so that the job of watching their little boy was split exactly fifty-fifty the whole time they were there.''

Daniel grabbed onto the train of thought like a drowning man. He just wished he could be certain of what she meant with her little parable. Say, just for conversation's sake, he *was* interested in marriage. He would be looking for a partner, someone to share life's joys and chores with, too, but right now that was taking things to an extreme. Daniel leaned back against a countertop and picked up a cookie, briefly critiquing the red-and-green-frosted jacket before biting off the head. He needed to retreat and think about things a bit. ''I ought to get going, Lu. It's getting late.'' He paused and decided to risk probing a bit farther. ''You don't think child care should be shared?''

Lucia leaned inside the refrigerator and retrieved a quart of milk. She poured them each a half glass and reached for a cookie herself. ''Here. You have to have a glass of milk if you're going to eat gingerbread.'' God knew she needed the liquids. Watching Daniel move around her kitchen had made her mouth go dry. ''Oh, absolutely. I just hate to see things so cut-and-dried. Everybody needs to be willing to give ninety percent to make things work.''

Taking a healthy swig of milk before neatly severing the neck scarf he had so carefully painted onto the ginger man from the rest of his body, Daniel questioned as he chewed, ''You don't think things should be set out in black and white as to what's expected of whom and when?''

She shivered. ''Too clinical.''

''I see.'' One arm and two raisin buttons disappeared. ''But if you don't talk it out beforehand and agree on at least the philosophy of how things should be handled, couldn't you find yourself married to somebody whose

views on marriage and commitment are diametrically op-
posed to your own?''

"Oh, I think you could sense that beforehand.''

"Do you really?''

"Don't you?''

"No.''

"Oh.'' She thought about that. "Why not?''

Because not everyone wore Lucia's rose-colored glasses.
People took advantage of one another. You needed to
protect yourself. Get it in writing that the other guy was
willing to put in as much effort as you were willing to.
There were a million becauses. It was a damn shame, but
those were the facts of the matter. Two people trying to be
successful and time at a premium read like a recipe for re-
sentment if you allowed yourself to get dumped on. After
all, a good offense was the best defense.

Daniel studied her through slitted lids. She was such a
curious mixture of woman and little girl. So trusting. She
would be easily hurt. Now, if *he* were to marry her, there
would be no need of a premarital agreement, clocks with
stopwatches or anything else. He would make sure nobody took advantage of her, including himself. "Life's a
two-way street, Lu...'' Had he said that? My God, clichés
were catching. "But sometimes people don't realize that.
They're caught up in their own world. Both partners need
to stake out a little space of their own.''

"Well, sure,'' Lucia agreed. "After all there're only
twenty-four hours in the day. You need some time to
yourself.'' She shrugged as she rinsed the soap off her
cookie sheets.

"I wasn't sure you were aware of that,'' Daniel interjected. "You seem to squeeze in more than twenty-four
hours' worth of activities into your days.''

"I have a lot of nervous energy to expend.''

"I guess."

"My mother likes to say that *you might as well fall flat on your face as lean too far backward*, but really, nothing I do is all that difficult."

Daniel considered again trying to unravel her thoughts, clarifying her earlier remarks, but thought better of it. Ordinarily the workings of Lucia's mind fascinated him. But it wasn't her mind giving his lower body fits right then. He had to get out of there. Leave the probing for another time. Decide what *he* wanted before worrying if she fit the bill. Take a cold shower. Important things.

"Walk me to the door."

"You're really leaving?" Lucia straightened from the countertop as Daniel draped an arm around her shoulders.

He stretched. "Yes. It's late. We can finish our debate another time."

"You don't have a car," Lucia pointed out.

That stopped him. "Mmm. That's right." Slowly, he turned. "I'll have to call a cab." He looked around expectantly. "Where's your phone?"

"In the bedroom." Lucia indicated the doorway to her right with a thumb.

Daniel sighed. The bedroom. It figured. The one room he'd tried to avoid like the plague. He absently brushed at the flour clinging to his good slacks as he entered the room in question. He stopped just inside the door. In his present state of mind, he was unsure as to what he'd expected of Lucia's boudoir. Probably black satin, red tassels, anything to explain the uncomfortable tightening in areas of his body gentlemen were taught not to mention in front of ladies.

He didn't get black satin, not even in an out-of-place brassiere carelessly hung over a dressing table chair. What he got were tall yellow tulips mixed with grape hyacinths that bloomed in trapuntoed profusion on the bedspread, a shirred white eyelet bed skirt and matching tiebacks on the window, pale jonquil-yellow walls and a lush green rug. The room was a patch of springtime, a warm welcome from the subzero windchill outside. Lucia's romanticism came out in the little subtle touches around the room. It was there in the flouncy skirt around the base of the dressing table, the fresh flowers on the nightstand near the four-poster bed and the antique celluloid comb and brush next to the old washbowl and pitcher on her bureau.

The living room was clean, cool and modern. A very downtown-type decor. The bedroom was the exact opposite. Daniel came to the conclusion that for all the logic the woman tried to employ, not only in her search for a husband but her rationale for choosing marriage in the first place, Lucia was a closet romantic.

Her growing list of necessary qualifications for husbandly material wouldn't matter a hoot nor a holler when the time came. She would simply go down for the count when she bumped into *him*. No muss, no fuss. It wouldn't matter if he was ten feet tall and made his living shoveling... manure. Daniel's office staff didn't need protecting from Lucia. If she thought Mr. Right was on his staff, she would have mowed over him by now. His company was safe, but what about him? How safe was he? How safe did he want to be? He would be better off trying to row a tin washtub across Lake Michigan in a gale than to stay any longer in her apartment if he wasn't interested in something long-term with Lucia. Lucia had a thing about marriage and commitment. He was developing a thing about Lucia. Ergo... he needed to get out of there.

Daniel shook his head in disgust and sat on the edge of the bed to make his phone call. Darned if he could figure where his head was in this mess. Unfortunately, his introspections caused his attention to be less than a hundred percent and he ended up knocking the small vase of fresh flowers off the nightstand and into his lap as he absently reached for the phone.

He jumped off the bed and pulled the spread back before the water soaked through to the sheets and mattress. He brushed at his pants with his hand and watched as all the flour that had clung to his pants turned to glue. He looked around for something to use for sopping up the water on the carpet and groaned. There was no way he was going out in the middle of a frigid winter night even if it was only as far as the curb and a taxi.

Lucia wandered in. She'd been back to the kitchen to see if the cookies were dry enough to stack. They had been and she'd done it. She was munching a leg that had broken off some poor little ginger soul when she came in. "Did you get through to the—oh, my." Her surprised mien took in a very uncomfortable-looking Daniel. "Whatever happened?"

"Don't ask."

So she didn't. Daniel expounded anyway.

"I knocked the damn vase over." He didn't tell her why he'd been distracted in the first place. "And then the water turned the flour on my pants into goo." The litany of complaints continued. "Why the hell didn't you have me use an apron or a towel, or *something* while we were baking?"

Lucia looked at him with her mouth hanging open. There was no way in blazes she was going to take responsibility for this one. He might be a foot and a half taller and outweigh her by more than a hundred pounds, but there were times when she absolutely refused to abide by her mother's axioms and this was one of them. Discretion being the better part of valor be darned.

She came out with both barrels blasting. "Now just a darn minute, buster." She actually poked him in the chest with her index finger, amazing him with her temerity. She was really something in a snit. The ability to focus all that passion in a different direction would give a man a reason to welcome the longer nights of winter. He found himself backing up, and Lucia followed right along, enjoying, in spite of her anger, the excuse for even limited contact. Every time she touched his chest with her fingertip, it was like wetting your finger and touching a battery. She got a buzz. When the backs of his knees hit the edge of her double bed, he sat down. His own frustrations gave way to a kind of amusement. She was really cute, although he was careful not to say so. He doubted "cute" would overly please her. But the fact of the matter was, she was kind of cute in any mood he'd found her in so far.

"You can hardly call me on the carpet because you didn't think to use an apron. I never use them. They cramp my style. All my stuff is machine washable and as easy to wash as an apron. You're all grown up," she pointed out. "If you wanted a towel or something, all you had to do was ask." Heck, she'd have volunteered to wrap it around his waist and tuck in the ends herself.

"I'll have to remember to do that," he replied mildly. He was content now to sit and let her tirade run its course.

She was still so wound up in the injustice of his accusations she didn't notice she had implied there would be a next time. It didn't slip by him.

"Furthermore, neither am I to blame for the fact that you're a klutz."

He stood, towering over her. She'd been close. Close enough to continue prodding him in the chest. His intimidating height was even more effective at that kind of range. She'd actually called him a klutz, and that was going too far, for he wasn't normally cloddy and was becoming a tad sensitive about the way thinking of her distracted him enough to turn him into someone a little less than coordinated.

Finally, noting the glare in Daniel's eye, Lucia decided it was best to retreat. She studied the pants, trying to figure out what in the world to do with them so that Daniel could at least get home. One thing for sure, he was going to have to take them off... and that was a fact that made her extremely ill at ease indeed. She swallowed nervously. "Listen," she said. "Why don't you go in the bathroom and hand me out the pants. I'll see what I can do with them. I don't suppose they're wash-and-wear?"

Daniel looked down and touched an experimental finger to the white flour glue covering the thighs of both legs. "Geez, I don't know. I always just send everything to the cleaners so they'll get a decent pressing." The results of his finger test clearly didn't please him, and he gave Lucia a pained look as he did his best to pull the wet fabric away from his leg.

"Well, just go get out of them and I'll see what I can do," she directed.

"Can you get me something to wrap up in?" Daniel requested. "I'm freezing."

After their "refreshing" walk to the Chicago Theater tonight, Lucia hadn't thought it possible for Daniel to get cold, but there was a first time for everything and he *was* starting to shiver a bit. She got him a flannel sheet from the new powder-blue-and-pink-floral-sprigged set she had just purchased for her bed and shooed him into the bathroom.

Fate can be cruel and the pants were wool. Lucia had to carefully rinse them in her sink while Daniel waited impatiently in her bedroom. This was not good. Here he was stuck in the one room he had no business being in if Lucia was to make it through the night still "respected." He couldn't stand all night. Finally, he sat on the edge of the bed, propped her pillow against the headboard and lay back. Hell, he would read. That would keep his mind off other, less respectable pursuits. Poor Lucia was probably entirely unaware of the fine line she walked tonight. If Daniel didn't get a tight grip on himself, she was going to have her hands full defending the virtue she was so sure nobody was interested in. Daniel began flipping through some of her nightstand reading. Lucia had eclectic taste, to say the least. Computer magazines and poetry anthologies were mixed in with the December *Good Housekeeping*. A megaromance, four inches thick, had her place marked with a recipe torn from a magazine. He settled in, interested in it all because she was.

Lucia was eventually able to rub the flour paste out of his pants and rinse them in cold clean water, but she couldn't put them in the dryer downstairs because they'd probably shrink. So she hung them over the shower rod. She hoped they would drip-dry during the few hours left before morning and he would be on his way with none of the neighbors any the wiser.

Her sleeves were still pushed up and her face flushed from the slight exertion when she reentered the bedroom. "I've gotten them as clean as possible," she informed him, eyeing the way he'd made himself at home on her double bed. "They're hanging in the bathroom as close to the radiator as I thought safe. It'll be a while, I'm afraid."

"Oh?" he asked idly as though the fact he had no pants on were of only minor consequence. He was determined not to make a further fool out of himself. "Nothing else to be done, I suppose." He shrugged.

She came forward and sat a little nervously on the opposite side of the bed, craning her neck to get a look at the article he was finding so fascinating. Here was a situation even her mother's myriad lectures had left uncovered. She'd try and adopt Daniel's blasé attitude.

Daniel had never figured himself as a candidate for sainthood, and now he knew why. His breathing and . . . other things really picked up when Lucia casually sat on the bed. Hadn't her mother taught her anything? He forced his attention back to the article and handed her the romance. "Here," he muttered. "Might as well read while we wait."

She was amazed. It was three o'clock in the morning, she was sharing the confines of her bed with a half-naked man—he'd taken off his shirt and tie, an action that left him in white cotton skivvies and her sheet—and she was supposed to *read* a romance? The guy in bed next to her was better looking, more virile and sexier than any hero she'd ever read about. If it was possible for a man to be larger than life, then Daniel was that man. She didn't want to read about some old pirate reduced to kidnapping a seventeen-year-old upper-crusty type who should have known better than to be out alone on the docks in the first place. Heck, she could be, wanted to be *living* her own romance. Here. Right now. This minute.

She wanted this particular hero to reach across that bed and grab her. Look deep into her eyes and do all the other corny things any hero throughout time had ever thought about doing to his lady. And she didn't want to think about cows giving their milk away, the plenitude of fish in the sea or how many more streetcars might be along after this one. Heck, how many of her mother's infamous streetcars were made by Cadillac like this one? And she certainly didn't want to use any of the certified-to-work, clever put-downs she'd spent so much of the past ten years of her life developing. She wanted to finally find out where the primrose path led.

Lucia looked across at the object of her dreams. He certainly looked totally engrossed in her computer magazine. She sighed. She didn't have the foggiest idea how to go about this; a cool—she refused to consider cold—shower would probably be better than embarrassing herself any further.

Quietly, well, sort of quietly—after all, it wasn't her fault if her hand slipped a little and the dresser drawer kind of slammed shut while she was getting her flannel nightie—she slipped from the room and down the short hall to the bath. She didn't take a long shower because she didn't want the humidity from the cascading water to interfere with the pants drying. But the dampness had been enough to curl a few blond tendrils into a loose frame for her face.

The flannel granny gown with its lace collar and cuffs added to the vulnerable air the wisps of hair lent, and Daniel was thoroughly disgusted with his instant response when she reappeared in the doorway.

"I called my folks," he said, trying to ignore the tightening in his groin. He was amazed that a woman covered from throat to ankle in flannel could cause him such discomfort. "Dad laughed himself silly, but they're not expecting me until morning now."

"Oh, that's good," Lucia said inanely. "Uh, Daniel."

"Yes?"

"I'd really like to get a few hours' sleep in before morning."

"It's practically morning now," Daniel pointed out. "Why don't we stay up reading for a while and watch the sun come up together?" He didn't think he could bear having her lying against him twice in one night; his good

intentions were rapidly sliding down the goodness scale.
Ten... nine... eight...

It certainly sounded romantic. Unfortunately, she had
this terrible pragmatic streak in her. "I haven't a window
that faces east. Even if I did, I'm afraid I'm just one of
those people who really needs their sleep." She moved a
little uncertainly into the room, eyeing both man and bed
longingly. It had been a long day. "I don't suppose I could
talk you into parking your magnificent body out on the
sofa in the other room?"

Daniel didn't even have to think about it. "The sofa's
way too short for me," he objected. "And it has lumps."
Seven... six... five...

She defended her choice in furniture. "It's old. New
furniture is expensive. I reupholstered that one myself."

"And it's very nice-looking," he soothed. "But not for
sleeping—at least not for someone my length."

He had her there. Sighing, she turned to troop out to the
living room herself.

"Where're you going?" he questioned.

She was surprised. "Why, to the living room, where
else?"

"No, no," he protested. "Stay here. It'll be fine, you'll
see." Oh, God. Four...three...two... "I'll just hold you
while you sleep." Sure he would. He didn't want to get
married. He didn't want to get married. He didn't—he
wondered if he'd believe the words if he repeated them
enough. Well, the Hilton, just around the corner from the
office, might be a nice place to host a rehearsal dinner and
he understood that was the groom's responsibility.

Lucia couldn't believe her ears. She'd just subjected
herself to a cold shower. Was he getting interested now?
"I'm not sure this is a good idea," Lucia murmured, but
she moved inexorably toward the bed, as if hypnotized.

Daniel lay quietly, watching her with gleaming magnetic eyes. There was no reason to break the silence while she moved in the direction he wanted. Finally, she reached the edge of the bed and looked a little uncertain. He smiled encouragingly.

She imagined a barracuda looked like that when it grinned. When he flipped down the spread, blanket and sheet, she eyed his expression warily, wondering *what* was going to happen next.

She pulled the sheet down the rest of the way, sat down and swung her legs in. Having never done this kind of thing before, she had absolutely no idea how to act. Truthfully, had it been anybody but Daniel lying there with gleaming predator eyes, she doubted she could have pulled it off at all. Daniel made her forget every snappy put-down she'd ever practiced. She carefully lowered her head onto the extra pillow and lay on her back, pulling the covers up to her chin as she did so. There. How brave could you get?

Daniel was already regretting suggesting they share the bed. His immediate reaction to her presence next to him only confirmed his suspicion that even in flannel, Lucia was deadly to him. Damn, she was potent. And he sensed her vulnerability to him, as well. That left him carrying a heavy load of responsibility...seeing that she wouldn't be hurt. They would talk and maybe he would hold her a bit. He would absolutely refuse to allow his baser instincts to dominate.

Daniel knew there would be gold stars for his heavenly halo earned tonight. He just hoped he would be able to hold his head up under their weight when he got up there. For the first time in his life, he was thinking about developing a permanent relationship...at least the abstract concept was appealing more and more, but his hands were tied, so to speak. So he lay there, wondering how far he could push his body without losing control, and what she would do if he pulled her onto her side and in to his body, spoon fashion.

The object of his thoughts lay stiffly on her back wondering when Daniel would initiate proceedings and getting more and more nervous as she did so. What if they got carried away? *Would* he respect her in the morning? What about her? How would she feel about herself?

"Lucia?" Daniel asked softly.

She jumped as though he had shouted. "What?"

Daniel set the magazine he'd been leafing through on the nightstand, turned on his side so he could look at her and propped his elbow on the bed and his head on his hand. "Tell me again why you want to get married."

Lucia felt at a distinct disadvantage, what with Daniel leaning over her like the grand inquisitor and herself flat on her back. So she kind of squiggled around a bit to end on her side facing Daniel, with her own head propped on a hand. He frowned, because now she was facing completely the wrong direction for spooning, and she misinterpreted the frown and became more nervous. "Well, uh, it's just that—"

"I mean," Daniel interrupted, "what's so bad about being single? Is marriage the only way your parents will see you all grown-up?"

At first, Lucia felt a flash of irritation at the negative connotations he was putting on what she saw as a relatively simple quest for a husband, and she flopped down on her back again to study the ceiling for inspiration. She'd never noticed before how she hadn't been quite steady with the paintbrush and had slopped dabs of wall color onto the white ceiling. Besides, why couldn't Daniel let that stupid quest thing drop? Right now the only man she wanted was asking fool questions about why she wanted to be married.

"I've got to tell you, Lu," Daniel continued, obviously having forgotten he'd asked her a question. "My parents seem happily married and all, but there have been guys I've known for years who I just don't see anymore. They're always too busy at home for old friends, you know? I really need to know how come you're so hot to get married. It sounds suffocating as all hell to me." Despite his words, Daniel sounded almost envious. And the fact was, he was starting to get an inkling of the forces at work. Forces strong enough to keep a man too busy for "the guys." They fascinated while they frightened.

To Lucia, he sounded envious and... bewildered. Well, he was no more so than she herself.

Chapter Nine

I guess I'm lonely," she said simply.

"Not possible," he contradicted, reverting to his old habit of verbal shorthand. Unable to resist, he brushed a few wayward tendrils off her forehead.

It was probably a good thing her brothers had been very overprotective when she was growing up. It was discouraging what an easy mark she was. Here he'd just virtually called her a liar, and she was fighting with herself to keep from moving in to his most casual of touches. She gave her head a slight shake to rid it of the lingering tingle his fingertips had caused. "I am so."

"How can you be?" Daniel asked in what he probably thought was a reasonable tone. To Lucia, he sounded the way she imagined he would in his chairman-of-the-board role. He then went on to list logically all the reasons he saw interfering with her claim of loneliness. "There's your food preparation business and all the people you meet there," he ticked off. "That alone takes up most of your

time away from work. There are the people you meet at
work itself. What about all the organizations you've joined
in your search for a mate? The church choir, the Statler
Club and the other ones I don't even know about. The
Christmas party alone took hours of time sequestered with
various eligible planning committee members.''

"Yes, but—''

But Daniel was not to be swayed. "Then there are all the
friends you've made in just the short period of time you've
been in Chicago. Good Lord, Tom and Roseanne are so
protective of you, I wouldn't be surprised if either one of
them took a swing at me next time I pick you up for
lunch.''

Lucia waved that objection away. "You're reading too
much into it. They're just annoyed because I used to feed
them all my leftovers. Now they have to fend for themselves.'' She lay on her side facing him and looked
thoughtful. "I really should clean out the refrigerator.
There's all kinds of stuff in there they could zap in the microwave rather than letting it go to waste.''

"You're digressing,'' Daniel warned.

"Cleaning the refrigerator fills in a lot of time,'' she
countered.

Daniel shook his head to clear it. "What are you talking about?'' he asked in too soft tones. The depressing part
was that he truly wanted to know. That didn't say much for
his sense of self-preservation.

She shrugged. He was fascinated by her granny gown's
gentle shimmy, especially on top. "Things like finding
homes for the leftovers instead of tossing them, screwing
doll buggies together instead of giving them unassembled,
all that stuff. Nonessential things. But they sure fill in a lot
of time that would otherwise be spent sitting around here
twiddling my thumbs all by myself.''

"But you *do* fill in the time," Daniel pointed out. "So how can you want to marry because of loneliness?" There had to be more to it than that.

Lucia flopped thoughtfully down onto her back again and the wall-mounted lamp over her bed flickered out. "Darn," she muttered as she reached over her head and fiddled with the little turnkey in the lamp's side for a few moments before getting the light back on. "Stupid, temperamental thing. You breathe hard in here and the dumb light goes out."

"So replace it," Daniel said, making what he thought was a reasonable comment, although he wasn't totally averse to the room's only light source being sensitive to the pressure of heavy breathing.

But Lucia looked askance. "My mother gave me that lamp," she exclaimed. "Once she realized I was serious about moving up here, she got me the lamp and a few other things for a housewarming present."

"It's not a house."

"It's as close as I'll get to one for a good long time. And now who's digressing? The point is, I can't just get rid of the lamp."

Daniel sighed. "Okay, so you refuse to replace a lamp that doesn't work. Fine. Let's get back to your claim of loneliness. I just don't see how it's possible."

But Lucia was having trouble concentrating. She had an irresistible urge to put her face in the healthy-looking patch of dark hair growing on Daniel's broad chest. There was just enough showing above the V-neck of his undershirt to be intriguing. She fought the impulse, although one hand strayed into the thicket in spite of her good intentions. "I can fill up time," she said as she tested the texture of the hair on his chest with her fingertips. "I'm very good at that. But there's always this empty space down here." She touched a spot approximately over her heart. "No matter how full I cram my days, it's only a distraction. That empty spot is always there to come home to."

Between the roving fingers on his chest and the hand pressing her gown down over her empty spot, which just happened to be right over her breasts, Daniel's breathing was beginning to get labored. The faulty lamp was sure to go off at any moment. "You expect a lot from marriage...from a man. I'm not sure if it's reasonable to expect a mere mortal to fill such deep needs. It seems to me you've got to be complete on your own and happy within yourself before you have anything to offer a permanent relationship. I mean, what does the guy get out of this?"

Lucia looked dreamy-eyed, not at all offended. "He gets *his* empty spot filled," she said and planted a kiss right in the middle of the silky thatch she'd been playing in for the past few minutes. His hair tickled her nose and she liked it. She just didn't know if Daniel did or not because he jumped when she did it. She came nearer, to examine it more closely. "It's mostly the holidays, I guess," she explained, blowing on the small visible patch. She liked that, too. "I want to buy our—my—" she hastily corrected "—kids crayons and lunch boxes in September. Make homemade Halloween outfits in October. And on Christmas..."

She absently smoothed over the thin cotton shirt covering his chest, and he tried to listen over the pounding of his heart.

"On Christmas I want my *own* family celebration. My parents go to my oldest brother's for Christmas dinner now. He's the only one with kids and that way they don't have to leave their gifts right after they get them. I get included in their invitation as an obligation. Mark and John and their wives don't come until dessert time. I hate being an obligation. I have a drawer full of neck scarves. Nobody's ever seen me wear one, but they have to get me something. So every year I get another silk scarf. Can't they see what a short neck I have and that a scarf makes it just about disappear?'' she asked rhetorically.

Daniel knocked scarves off his list of possible Christmas gifts for Lucia and examined her neck. It looked okay to him. In fact, as far as he was concerned, it was one great-looking neck. No wonder she didn't want to camouflage it with scarves.

Lucia shivered when Daniel lightly traced its length. The downy hairs at her nape stood at attention when his hand passed over them, and he wrapped the blankets more tightly around her when he noticed the tremor passing through her. ''I want to be up at three o'clock on Christmas morning screwing little red wagons together.''

''It'd take you that long, too,'' Daniel teasingly interjected, ''if you don't break down and get yourself a screwdriver. Quarters are not terribly efficient for anything other than parking meters.''

She gave him a speaking look. ''I want to buy black patent shoes and dresses with yards of eyelet on them for Easter Sunday. Froufrou hats dripping with ribbon and fake daisies. Red, white and blue crepe paper to decorate bicycle spokes on the Fourth of July. And I want to march in the rain in the Memorial Day parade with a Cub Scout den or a Brownie troop.''

Daniel's worries increased. It sure sounded to him as though Lucia thought personal fulfillment came part and parcel with marriage. He knew for a fact it wouldn't work. You had to like yourself and be internally at peace before you could find happiness. Then you'd have it whatever the circumstances. A husband couldn't give it to you. Babies couldn't give it to you. ''It'd be simpler to volunteer at the Cradle Society.''

Surprise colored her features. As pillow talk, his con-
versations left a lot to be desired. Here they were in bed
together, and he was sending her off to work with home-
less children? She hadn't had much personal experience,
but she'd read a lot. This was the *strangest* seduction attempt she'd ever been privy to, bar none. She looked at
him thoughtfully. Provided of course, that was what it
was. She was beginning to doubt her mother's hard-and-
fast belief in the male's one-track mind, at least where this
male was concerned. He didn't look at all ready to pounce
on her nubile young body. Yes, he was giving her the shivers, but the caresses that were doing her in seemed to be all
absentmindedly given. Sort of a natural need to touch
rather than a studied seduction attempt. "Oh, I don't
think so. That would be like working in a candy shop
where no sampling was allowed."

Having kids wouldn't necessarily prevent loneliness,
Daniel knew. Some of his friends' kids specialized in being
perverse. And what happened when they turned adoles-
cent and preferred their peer group to their parents? No,
loneliness was internal as far as he was concerned. "You
can be lonely in the middle of a crowd, you know," he
said.

Lucia looked at him strangely, not really grasping his
point. "Yes, I know," she responded politely. "Isn't that
what I was just pointing out as a key reason for why I
wanted to find a husband? So I wouldn't be lonely in the
middle of a crowd?" He was in the strangest mood tonight. So philosophical.

He closed his eyes in exasperation. She just didn't get it.
She had to realize that changing her external situation—
running away from Chillicothe, having a husband and
family—none of that would take away her loneliness,
which sprang only from her herself. You could be lonely

not only in a crowd of acquaintances, but also surrounded by loved ones. Externals could change all they wanted, but it was what was *inside* that counted when it came to loneliness.

He sighed and decided to give up for the evening. Suddenly, it was too much to handle at . . . four in the morning. Four o'clock? Lord, he hadn't been up this late since his senior-year calculus final. He'd pulled an all-nighter, falling asleep at six in the morning for a quick nap only to sleep right through the exam. His professor had not been pleased.

He reached for Lucia and she wondered if the seduction was about to take place, but he merely turned her to her opposite side and pulled her flannel-clad body back to his chest and snuggled up to her.

The slight movement involved caused the light to go out. Daniel grunted but didn't complain. After all, he'd just been saved the effort of turning it off himself.

Lucia smiled as she began to drift off to sleep. Sleeping next to Daniel was like backing up to a warm furnace. She'd never been so comfortable in her life.

She turned slightly to tell him that. Her mouth was open and ready to go, in fact, when the doorbell rang.

For a moment, she froze. Amazement etched her features as she looked from her clock radio's eerily glowing green numerals to Daniel's face and back to the radio again: 4:14. "Who can that be?" she whispered as though not wanting to be heard by whoever lurked down the hall, through the living room and on the other side of her solid oak front door.

"Well, don't look at me," Daniel whispered. "It's *your* apartment, after all."

Lucia sat up in bed and worked with the temperamental light for a few seconds before she got it back on. She worried her bottom lip with her teeth while she thought. "Should I answer it?"

"What do you normally do?" Daniel asked politely. He wouldn't have been surprised to hear that this was a run-of-the-mill occurrence, like the milkman, stopping by for breakfast.

The bell buzzed again, and Lucia grew more agitated. She nervously clasped the satin binding on the blanket, shifting awkwardly beneath it. "This's never happened before," she said, looking anxiously in the direction of the front door.

Daniel felt a rush of relief upon hearing that. However, he couldn't help but wonder how she would handle it, now that the occasion had arisen. "What do you *think* you should do?" he asked in an old managerial ploy. "What are your options?"

Lucia found it difficult to think clearly at the moment. "Geez, I don't know." She looked ready to wring her hands. "Maybe we should call the police," she offered hopefully, leaning over him in a grab for the phone.

With a sigh he put his hand over hers, staying the call to Chicago's finest. "Lucia, you're not alone tonight." Thank the good Lord he was there to protect her. "I'm here."

She interrupted. "Yes, but they might have a gun or something." After all, big bodies were nice for moving large boxes and such, but they would stop a bullet with no more finesse than smaller ones.

"I'm not suggesting that you invite them in for tea and cookies, Lu. But you do have a peephole. Go use it and see who it is. Don't open the door, just find out who they are and what they want, okay?"

It sounded reasonable to her. She left the bed and made her way down the hall. Good grief, whoever was doing the knocking either was using a club or had one heck of a set of knuckles. Actually, she knew an entire family like that, but they were three hours away just outside of Peoria. She crept through the darkened living room and nervously called out, "Yes, who is it?"

In the bedroom, Daniel was in somewhat of a pickle. He didn't like Lucia handling this on her own, but parading through the house in little more than a floral sheet didn't hold much appeal, either. "Damn," he swore under his breath as he heard the chain sliding on the front door. All the woman had to do was tell whoever it was they had the wrong apartment or that her husband was in the other room phoning the police, something...anything to get rid of them. But not Lucia. Oh, no. It was probably the lunatic that his mother had fainted on top of at the theater, and Lucia was inviting him in for coffee, gingerbread and a lecture on the evils of alcohol. He wouldn't put it past her.

He pulled the sheet around him like a toga. It was going to be tough to be properly intimidating in flower-sprigged Roman wear, but he would give it his best shot. He lumbered off the bed, a bear with a thorn to excise. There was more than one deep voice out there. Hell, what had she done, invited the Chicago Bears' front line in for a pre-dawn snack? His irritated movements caused the finicky light to flicker once in protest and then go out. Daniel cast a few aspersions on the ancestral tree of the factory workers responsible for its assembly as he groped his way across the floor. He managed to stub his toe on the end of the bed, which put an evil scowl on his already annoyed features. It was perfect for scaring away potential home invaders.

Not this home. Not this evening.

"Lucia," he thundered as he marched down the hall and into the living room, "what in holy hell is going on? What are you thinking of letting a bunch of men—" he got his first good look at the group in the room as he rounded the corner "—in at this time of the morning?" Reality hit home and Daniel turned from glowering at Lucia to really take in the four giants dwarfing her front room.

"Good God," he muttered. For as unusually large as Daniel was, these giants were of almost equal timber... and there were *four* of them.

The four spoke as one, and at the same time as Daniel.

"Lucia, who are these people?"

"Lu, who is this guy?" They gave Daniel a scowl at least as intimidating as his own and then simultaneously tacked on, "And what's he doing in your apartment at this time of night—" they looked him up and down "—undressed?"

Lord, Daniel had found himself in all kinds of circumstances in his time, but leave it to Lucia to come up with this nightmarish twist. "Lucia..." He drawled her name out threateningly.

Lucia still couldn't think clearly. She tried a weak laugh. Everyone knew laughter knocked the kinks out of the chain of life. Glancing around the room, she decided to call home and have her mother drop that one off her list. Lucia's personal chain of life was developing more kinks than a Slinky in full snarl.

"Uh, Daniel." She looked uncertainly from his still rather fierce scowl to the four matching scowls reflecting back from just inside her front door. She took a deep breath. "Daniel, I'd like you to meet my brothers, Matthew, Mark and John. And my father, Harvey?" There was a slight rise in her voice at the tail end, as though she were questioning the relationship she had just an-

nounced. Nervously, she wound a long blond strand
around an index finger. The tension was so thick in her
front room, you could cut it with a knife. Her gaze sought
out Daniel.

Matthew, Mark, Lucia and John? Oh brother, only
Lucia would come from a family like that. Daniel's stance
remained wary. His eyes shifted from the grim foursome
across the way to the nervous female in the middle. "Your
family lives in Chillicothe," he pointed out, as though
they'd grown roots there that made it impossible for them
to ever escape the place. God, please don't let this be her
father and brothers he was meeting while wrapped up like
a spring bouquet awaiting delivery. His prayers went un-
answered.

"We drove up soon as the diner closed," grunted one.

"Mama said she wasn't comin' home for Christmas,"
said a second.

The third allowed, "Always been there before. Mom's
mighty upset." He cleaned a fingernail with the index finger of the opposing hand and went on in a most accusing
way, "We came up to *reason* with Lucia, but now I'm
thinking... you got anything to do with any of this?"

God help him. He'd upset Mom. Any other embarrassing situation Daniel had ever been in paled next to this one.
He felt all of seventeen. In fact, having Mary Ellen Ebie's
father catching them necking on her darkened front porch
with his hand edging under the hem of her pink angora
sweater hadn't been nearly this bad. At least he'd had his
pants on back then. Oh, well, at least his presence would
keep the *reasoning* from getting too heavy-handed. He
hoped.

Daniel thought it was Matthew, but it might have been
Mark, who repeated his earlier question. "Who is this guy,
Lucia?"

"I'd like you all to meet Daniel Statler." Lucia introduced Daniel primly, as though they had just bumped into
each other at a black-tie function. "Daniel, my family,"
she finished simply.

Daniel followed her lead. "How do you do?" he asked.
He offered the hand not holding the sheet in place.

John, or possibly Mark, checked his wrist and questioned darkly, "What's he doing here at this time of the
morning?"

Daniel's outstretched hand was ignored. He recognized
that they were pros at intimidating Lucia's suitors.

"Statler? Isn't that the name of the company where you
work? Is this guy your boss?"

Lucia seemed at a loss to understand the growing fur-
rows of her brother's brows. If they dipped much deeper
they would totally obscure their vision. "Well, uh, yes,"
she said, nodding. "Daniel is the owner of Statler Computing Group." She wondered why they weren't pleased
that she was dating a company president. Hadn't Mom
always said it was as easy to fall in love with a rich man as
a poor one?

Daniel attributed her puzzled look to the naïveté he
found so refreshing and frustrating. Unfortunately, the
brothers didn't seem to suffer the same lack of cynicism.
They looked anything but innocent. He closed his eyes and
shook his head. Here came the grand inquisition.

He wasn't disappointed. "Lucia," one of them began—Daniel had no idea which one. "How many times
has Mom told you that *a man won't buy the cow if he can
get the milk for free*? Surely by now you know the difference between the kind of girl a guy'll sleep with and the
kind he'll marry." Whoever it was turned heavily on Daniel. "And as for you, if you're holding her job over her

head for a little easy sex, we won't wait to sue you. We'll draw and quarter you right here and now."

"You can try," Daniel responded in a soft but firm voice. Hell. He was willing to put up with a certain amount of grief. After all, the present circumstances would look suspicious to the casual onlooker. But, come on! Holding her job over her head for sex? Holding anything over Lucia's head for any reason whatsoever? These guys didn't know their sister very well. Or Daniel.

"It's not like that!" Lucia quickly interjected as the two sides faced off. Her brothers looked amazed at her interruption. She didn't blame them, since their heavy-handed intimidation had always worked before. After all, they'd been big, strapping full-sized men facing down half-grown adolescents. But Daniel was as old and as large as her brothers. She suspected he wouldn't react well to intimidation. It would be four against one, and Daniel might be hurt. She couldn't abide that and stepped between them all.

Her father—Daniel knew it was her father because he was the only one with gray hair and a bald spot—said, "Lucia, your Mom wants you home for Christmas. Go pack your bag while your brothers and I explain the facts of life to your Mr. Statler. You been up here long enough to prove your point. It's time to come home." He actually spit on his hands and rubbed them together in preparation for a little good old-fashioned fisticuffs.

Daniel gave a grim little smile. Fine. Her brothers and her dad couldn't be bothered to listen to her explanations. No wonder she'd left home. Well, he'd grown up on the south side of Chicago. If he went down, it would be in a blaze of glory. "Lucia, you don't have to go with them if you don't want to." He noticed she was still standing fearfully between the two factions. "But you really do have to move. Go on in the other room. I can handle this."

Lucia looked panic-stricken. Good God, they were going to fight right there in her living room. "If you'd all just listen—"

"Lucia, leave the room." The directive came from all sides.

"Seriously, I—"

"*Lucia*, leave the room!"

She couldn't allow them to hurt Daniel and took a deep breath in preparation for further rebuttal.

"*Lucia, leave the room!*" It was a chorus. Her dad, her brothers, even Daniel, all in perfect harmony.

Well, tough tootsies. Nobody, not even her family, would hurt her man while she had breath in her. "No," she said. "I won't." And she planted herself more firmly in front of Daniel, and even spread her arms a bit as if to protect him from all comers.

Her family looked shocked at her change of allegiance. But Daniel was delighted. Little Lucia, who'd left home rather than face up to her overprotective siblings and parents was finally doing it now...and for him! He was flabbergasted, pleased and frightened. Here was the bare beginning of what could be a partnership. Two people willing to put themselves on the line for each other. Of course, it was laughable to think of Lucia succeeding in holding off four hulks like her father and brothers to save Daniel's hide, but it made him humble that she was willing to try. Did she realize what she was doing? Did he even

want to fan the flames of this newfound discovery? He'd
certainly gotten himself into a fine mess this time!

"I expect you all to take my word that nothing happened here tonight."

Daniel stood behind her, wary and still ready but enjoying watching Lucia take on the protective role. She
looked regal, haughty and adorable.

"No, really," she protested when they looked doubtfully at her. She talked quickly now. At least she had their
attention. "We were baking cookies. You can even have
some. There're a few extra that I don't need. Daniel got
flour all over his pants."

"You were baking cookies at this time of the morning?" she was asked incredulously by her father.

"Well, yes. *Idle hands are the devil's workshop*, you
know. We were keeping our hands busy. So they didn't get
us into trouble." Her mother would have gone for that.
She wasn't so sure about her father and brothers.

Daniel groaned and covered his eyes. It was debatable
which was worse. Having them think he was staying overnight for the typical male reasons, or having them think he
was a nerd who baked cookies at the crack of dawn to keep
himself out of trouble.

At her brothers' doubtful looks, Lucia rambled on.
Daniel considered stopping her mouth with a kiss, but
quickly thought better of it. "I mean, I'm a secretary, for
crying out loud. In personnel. Good grief, I could get a job
like that anyplace I wanted. What's there to coerce me
with?" She looked appealingly at her family, still blocking Daniel off.

Oh, good. So now it wasn't that he wasn't capable of using his female employees in the worst possible way, but only that in Lucia's particular case it wasn't worth his while to do so. Fine and dandy. Daniel turned to leave the room.

"Where are you going?" Lucia questioned worriedly.

"To see if my pants are dry," he grunted.

"I don't see how they could be," she said with an apologetic look at Daniel. "It hasn't been long enough."

"Just how long has he been here pantless?" her father asked. His brows collapsed back down over his eyes.

Daniel shook his head in exasperation.

"Just what in bloody hell did we interrupt? What kind of gingerbread baking gets a man's pants soaked through?"

Daniel had trouble working a few words in edgewise. He couldn't seem to move fast enough to cut Lucia off. He noted the paucity of hair on top of Lucia's dad's head. That's what a lifetime of living with Lucia could do to a man.

"He just knocked a flower vase into his lap and the flour that had been there turned to goop. We tried to sponge it off, but..." She shrugged to show the inexplicability of the event.

"And *who* did the sponging off of the front of his pants, Lucia?" a brother questioned. From the look on his face, he was beginning to enjoy the discomfiture of his sister's giant boyfriend. "You or him?"

"Matthew..."

So that one was Matthew. That left only Mark and John to be tagged.

"Don't be indelicate," Lucia scolded.

At the expression on Matthew's face, Daniel almost hooted out loud, but thought better of the matter.

All the brothers seemed to be relaxing a bit, as it became obvious to them that although their baby sister had come to the big city, she hadn't *become* big city. Daniel could almost see the collective sigh of relief being breathed. Her dad's complexion seemed to be improving as well, although he still looked far from pleased.

"I'm not the one making excuses for a boyfriend without pants," Matthew pointed out. "As far as I'm concerned, that makes you two the indelicate ones. What do you think, Mark?"

Daniel was then able to identify a second brother. "Oh, indubitably." Mark joined in the fray. "Lucia, you know what Mom says about people in glass houses casting stones. I hardly think you're in any position here to be questioning Matthew's delicacy."

"That's right, Lucia,"—it had to be John—chirped in. Daniel edged out of the room in the middle of the debate to finish checking on the offending article of clothing. He could well understand why Lucia had left home. Her family could be a bit overwhelming. Lucia's mother would probably have something original to say, like the brothers never rained, they poured. He must remember to thank his parents for leaving him an only child.

He noticed the rumpled bed and darkened bedroom on his way down the hall. He shut the door and sent up a prayer. "Please God, don't let them notice this until I'm out of here. You and I know nothing happened, but they'd never believe it."

At the end of his tether, Daniel slipped into the bathroom. Clammy or not, the pants were going back on his body.

When she noticed the bathroom light switch on, Lucia smiled apologetically at her family and backed down the hall. Her brothers stood grinning and watching from the living room as she stood outside the bathroom door and whispered to its occupant, "What are you doing, Daniel? You can't wear wet pants in this weather. You'll catch your death of cold."

"This entire situation is straight out of Ripley's." His voice was clearly audible through the door. "I haven't felt this dumb since I was prepubescent."

"Don't be silly. It's all in your mind. They're very understanding. Really."

Yeah, and pigs flew. She'd virtually run away from home to get away from all their "understanding." "Look, just go back out there and entertain your family, okay?" He was beginning to feel decidedly desperate.

"But how will you get home? There's still the problem with the car," she questioned.

"I'll walk, if necessary."

"This time of night? It's not safe."

She was right, but in Daniel's current mood, the question was, not safe for whom? Daniel or a potential mugger? "Tough." That was certainly succinct.

As usual, Lucia couldn't leave well enough alone. "My family can give you a ride."

He was horrified. "Absolutely not!" That was just what he needed!

But Lucia had the bit between her teeth in her new-found role of protectress. She insisted John drive Daniel home. There was more of her mother in her than she'd ever suspected.

Daniel was sure he'd lost all control over his life. He insisted otherwise and vowed to himself never to see her again.

Chapter Ten

Daniel lasted through Monday and half of Tuesday. At eleven-thirty on Tuesday morning he broke down and called personnel. The phone rang three times and then he heard the click as the call was transferred to a nearby desk just as it was programmed to do when not answered at the original station. Lucia must be away from her desk. A very distracted Roseanne finally answered.

"Personnel, Ms. Thackeray."

"Roseanne, it's Daniel."

"Daniel, how are you?"

"Fine," he responded impatiently. "Just fine." There was the sound of papers being turned as he spoke. "Where's Lucia?"

"Hmm?"

"Lucia," he enunciated. "Where is she?"

"Oh, she's not here." More shuffling.

Daniel ground his teeth and prayed for patience. Roseanne was a very good director of personnel. Losing her over Lucia would be the crowning blow. "I know that, Roseanne. She didn't answer her phone. Has she taken an early lunch, or is she just away from her desk for a minute?"

Unfortunately for Daniel's peace of mind, Roseanne's thoughts were elsewhere. "Umm, no. She's gone. Listen, Daniel, about this sick-leave policy you wanted clarified . . ."

Daniel didn't care a fig about the new sick-leave policy just then. He wasn't sure he really cared about *anything* business-related at all anymore. Was he losing his touch already? Burned out at thirty-four? How depressing. He came from a very long-lived family. Regardless, it was somehow more important to find Lucia just then, and Roseanne's "gone" had a very ominous ring to it.

"Roseanne, let's talk about sick leave later. Where in hell has Lucia gone *to*?" Something told him it wasn't the powder room.

"Someplace exotic, I hope. She sounded upset when she called in yesterday."

Daniel sat back up in his chair. "She hasn't been in at all?"

"No."

Daniel braced himself.

"Actually, she said she was quitting. I talked her into time off instead. She's so darn good at what she does that I don't want to lose her. She'll be back, Daniel. Not to worry."

"She didn't say where she was going?" he persisted.

"Nope. Just that she was going. Is there a problem with her taking some vacation time right now?"

Daniel flopped back in his chair, flummoxed. "Maybe she decided to go home for the holidays after all," he thought out loud. It was possible her family had talked her into it after he'd left. Thursday was Christmas. She could have decided to take the whole week. He sat back up and began drumming the desk top with his best gold pen. "She'll be back Monday?" The week stretched out interminably before him because Lucia wasn't there to fill it.

"She didn't say that," Roseanne admitted over the wires. "I got her to agree that it wouldn't be too long. And she promised to help pick out the new computer system you've okayed for the office when she got back, since she'll use it the most."

A very puzzled Daniel hung up the phone several minutes later. His thoughts were tumultuous. He sat back in his chair again, twirling his pen and catching it to drum the desk top again in one of his flashiest old collegiate drumstick spins while he tried to make order out of the chaos in his brain. The facts were that Lucia had taken off, giving no destination and no real promise of return. What about her catering business? She'd begged off the trip to Racine with him because her clients *depended* on her so. What about them?

She'd *said* she wanted to marry partially because she was tired of lonely holidays. So she took off by herself the week of Christmas? Daniel snorted where he sat. What a Lucia-like thing to do.

It only made sense if she were trying to get away from something. Like what? He doubted she was even aware his interests had taken a more domestic turn lately. There'd been no time to discuss it. Daniel sat up slowly in his chair, his posture suddenly perfect. There was one other remote possibility. Her father and brothers were...large. And interfering. They'd also taken Mom's displeasure *very* seriously...

He thought more about it. On top of that, that entire group of said people hadn't been happy to find him in the apartment with her. He could easily see their protective instincts taking over and bodily removing her from harm's way. After all, *they* had no way of knowing that he knew Lucia was not the kind you fooled around with and then walked away from. He could easily imagine—in vivid Technicolor—that phalanx of ex-football types carrying his Lucia kicking and screaming down to their car. His Lucia, an unwilling kidnap victim. Oh my God!

Love might be blind, but Daniel was seeing red. Slapping the desk with the palm of his hand, he rose. He was going after her. He would get to the bottom of this mess and then he would propose, by God. And if his song of love wouldn't play just outside Peoria, he would kidnap her himself until she came to her senses and gave up her search for a shrimp.

His hands clenched, he rose heavily from his chair and began to pace. Would it work? Was there even a possibility? There was a certain unrealness about Lucia, a fairytale quality that was part of what charmed him. She was Cinderella looking for her prince and wanting to live happily ever after.

Daniel stopped in his tracks, his eyes narrowed. He was no damn Prince Charming, that was for sure. And there wasn't a lot he could do about his size or his personality, either. Since there was no fairy godmother available to turn him into the man of her dreams, happily ever after could get a little rocky.

There in the middle of the room, Daniel reached a decision. It was time for Lucia to stop using logic in her search for true love.

There was no logic to love.

He was too tall. She was too short. Her head was up in the clouds. His feet were so firmly attached to the ground they were growing roots. The list could go on, but had lost its point when Daniel realized his strong conviction that however arduous the compromises, he and Lucia could handle them. After all, they would have love on their side.

Daniel stopped his pacing in the middle of the room. A small smile played around his strongly chiseled lips as he thought of Lucia's attempts to apply the principles of logic to her husband hunt. Aristotle was, no doubt, rolling over in his grave.

But what was Daniel's excuse? He was a master at flowcharting and logic. It was what made him so good at what he did. He sighed. Lord, life was complicated. Where did he get off criticizing her ideas of marriage and love? Hadn't his own been just as unreal? She was a romantic and expected marriage to work. He tended toward the cynical and expected it to fail. Hell, all he had to do was read the papers to know that the divorce rate was sky-high. They would find a middle ground. They had to.

He leaned back against the massive highly polished wooden desk that dominated that portion of the room and rubbed the bridge of his nose. Her brothers and father had definitely *not* approved of his presence in her apartment at four in the morning. The only thing saving him from annihilation had been the evidence of the wet pants. His eyes narrowed. He'd gone off and naively left Lucia in their clutches, assuming her safe in the bosom of her family. But now they were gone, and so was Lucia. His chest swelled at the injustice of the situation.

The most important thing he had to do was find his wood sprite. It was tough to convince an empty room of his undying devotion. He had to go down there. He sighed and set his pen down on the desk top behind him. Nothing like a little romantic confrontation with the prospective in-laws to make a man's day. First he had to get her address. But he wouldn't call first. Driving down and just showing up at their door would catch them off guard and be more effective.

Whoever would have thought he had such a streak of romanticism, Daniel thought to himself wryly. He felt like

Ivanhoe going off to save Rebecca from the clutches of the wicked Brian.

Only Rebecca wasn't there to be saved.

Lucia's mother, another very tall person, looked more than a little surprised to be confronted by a dour, determined-looking man and have it be demanded that her baby daughter be released from captivity. But after more than four hours of driving on winter-glazed slippery highways and narrow secondary roads, Daniel was in no mood to be tactful.

"Lucia hasn't seen fit to darken my doorway in three solid months," the woman informed him. "She'll be amazed by how I've grayed since her last visit. I'm really quite irritated that she's not coming home for Christmas."

"So we figured when you sent your troop of goons to storm her apartment."

A light came on in her eyes, and Daniel knew she had figured out who he was. She didn't give an inch. "Lucia belongs in the bosom of her family." And she crossed her arms over her own rather large one, daring him to disagree.

My God. She really *did* talk in clichés.

"After all, *home is where the hearth is* and the Callahan hearth is right here." She pointed to the small diner's floor. "What can she accomplish up there that couldn't be done right here with her family and friends about her—besides getting into trouble?"

He wouldn't touch that line with a ten-foot pole. "Lucia is an adult now, over twenty-one," he began.

Her mother sniffed. "Age is as age does."

Not only did she talk in clichés, she twisted them to her own purposes. "She's made many new friends who care a great deal for her and has her own food-preparation business that is doing quite nicely.'' Daniel bragged quite openly without realizing it was a silly thing to do to Lucia's own parent. "She's picking out new computers and reorganizing the entire personnel department of my company.''

"She belongs *here*," Edna Callahan insisted.

"Not against her will!" Daniel exploded back, losing his patience entirely. "You can't hog-tie her and carry her off against her will!"

Edna was indignant. "Nobody hog-ties my baby. Certainly not her own brothers."

"Really? Then how is it she's disappeared after a predawn visit from your husband and sons?''

Edna Callahan studied Daniel's face for a few minutes, and her expression gradually changed from pugnaciousness to concern. Daniel could only assume that on top of everything else, he'd lost his poker face. Now every businessman he tried to negotiate with would be able to read him like a book. Great.

"Harvey," Edna called as she turned back into the kitchen portion of the diner. "That fellow you were talking about says Lu hasn't been home since the weekend! He's worried about foul play!''

"No," Daniel whispered. "That's not what I said." He made an effort to keep his voice down. They had the attention of everyone in the diner by that point. Mrs. Callahan was the quintessential mother figure. Her little darling was being threatened by forces unknown and Mom was gearing up for a full-scale invasion. "I said she wasn't there *now*. She called in Monday morning and gave her supervisor some line about needing to get away or some such thing...." His voice trailed off as Edna turned and gave him a look. Clearly, she was unimpressed with his mental prowess.

"If she called in early Monday, how could we have kidnapped her and carried her off Saturday morning?" she demanded to know.

She had him there. "I didn't actually talk to her," he explained rather weakly. "As I said, the supervisor down in personnel..."

Edna sniffed—she had an incredible repertoire of sniffs, Daniel was learning—and turned back to her husband, who had emerged from the kitchen with a skillet of sizzling...something. "Lu's gone off without so much as a 'how d'you do' and the stormer of her castle here has found himself up against empty walls. What do you make of that?"

Daniel went rigid as all eyes in the diner turned back to him, and he wished devoutly for the power to redo the past few hours. Harvey looked thoughtful, and the...whatever they were...sizzled a little less intensely. "She couldn't have called if she were lying dead in some Chicago back alley," he allowed. "Kidnappers would have been asking for ransom by now, so I guess we'll have to take her word that she needed some time to herself." He pierced Daniel with his sharp gray gaze. "Question is, why?"

"Why what?" Daniel countered, not liking the look of battle flaring to life in both of the protective parents.

"Why'd she feel the need to get away from that wonderful new life she's always carrying on about?"

Both Callahans took a step closer and spoke in unison. "What'd you do?"

Daniel's face was the picture of wounded innocence, however contradictory the look seemed on his chiseled features. "What did *I* do?" he exploded. "Why she's been a thorn in my side from the moment I first met her trying to screw a baby buggy together with a quarter."

"Baby buggy?" There was now real menace in Lucia's parents' voices, and they took *two* steps forward. They were practically on top of Daniel.

And for the first time in God knew how many years, Daniel actually backed a step away from a threat. "Yes, baby...no, not *that* kind of baby buggy. See, it was the night before the company Christmas party, and she was trying to assemble toy buggies." Her parents didn't look terribly convinced. "For the employees' kids' presents," he stressed. "From the Statler Santa." He breathed a sigh of relief when their grim looks softened ever so faintly. He got the impression he had just had a very narrow escape.

"So why'd she take off if she doesn't have a bun in the oven?" There was determination behind Edna's irate features.

He had to think for a minute. Bun in the oven? Bun in— "Oh...no. She's not pregnant! You mustn't think, she would never...I would never..." Didn't they know their own daughter better than that? Couldn't they tell how he felt about her? He certainly *felt* transparent enough. Thank God they'd gotten cold feet that night. The thought of facing this duo with news of wrong-side-of-the-blanket impending grandparenthood had Daniel virtually in hives. The stone facade was well and truly cracked. Daniel sighed and sat heavily in the booth he had been backed up against. He ran his huge hands through his hair in an uncharacteristic distracted gesture that left tufts sticking out at odd angles, and in a rather subdued voice asked if he might have a cup of coffee. Edna sat across from him as though to keep guard and Harvey dropped off his skillet in the kitchen with the other cook when he picked up the coffee. "Ruined," he grunted.

Then, in another first for Daniel, he sat for forty-five minutes trying to explain his feelings to Lucia's parents.

The three of them went through two pots of coffee, and Daniel was starting to feel a little wired. "It's so unlike me," he stated. "I always know my own mind. Then I met Lucia," he said, as though that explained everything. He shook his head in despair. "I've decided, though. She'll probably never make a good corporate wife. She's too real and doesn't know how to play games. But she's what I need for me, myself. And now she's gone. I'm so confused."

"Lu'll do that to you," Harvey spoke sagely, as though discussing a mind-altering drug rather than his daughter. "She's had her mother'n me goin' in circles since the day she insisted on bein' born three months before she should've."

Edna concurred. "That's the truth. Been determined to do things her own way ever since, too." She looked chagrined as she said, "That little girl gave me more gray hair than the three boys combined, and that's gospel." Edna sat back thoughtfully. She studied Daniel before saying slowly, "We'll help you find her, though. But it won't exactly be an act of charity," Edna warned. "She wore us to a frazzle with some of her antics. But I got a feeling you can handle it. You'll have to, 'cuz I can see you got it bad." At his questioning look, she explained. "Love. It's like the measles. Can't have it but once, and the older you are, the tougher it goes." She looked pleased with herself.

Daniel grimaced. He would have to stay on his toes to stand a chance around Mom. Besides, it wasn't that he wanted to *look a gift horse in the mouth*, but he didn't see how Edna and Harvey would be able to find Lucia. It was a big country out there, and she could be anywhere in it. "Even if we *could* find her, she might not want me. She has a list, you know. A list of husbandly attributes she's looking for. And I don't have too many of them, either, if you must know."

Harvey nodded as if he expected nothing less. "She would, and you wouldn't," he agreed. "You're too big and too determined. There'd be a lot of compromisin', no doubt about that." He looked introspective before nodding his head as if he had made up his mind. He rose from the wine-colored vinyl booth, wiping his hands on the big white apron covering his front. "You're strong. Strong enough to be gentle with my Lu. It won't be easy, though. She was a case and a half when she was growing up. One harebrained stunt after the next. And never willing to take any blame on her own doorstep. Nope. She always said we were pickin' on her because of her size." He gave a short crack of laughter. "Blamed every battle she ever lost on our size advantage. Sort of a 'might making right,' you might say. Truth was, we needed every advantage we *had* to stay one step ahead of her." The big man stood thoughtfully by the table. "And maybe we *were* a bit overprotective. We coddled her. But she wasn't strong as a child, just stubborn. Refused to admit she had limits. I'll never forget the day she was born, not as long as I live. All those doctors hovering over the most pathetic excuse for a newborn you'd ever hope to see...tubes running everywhere.

"Well, she doesn't need us now. She's strong. Physically and underneath where it counts most." Absently, Harvey used his one hand to knock a few crumbs off the small tabletop into the other hand. "Thing is," he confessed. "It's real hard to turn it off...the protecting, that is." He cleared his throat. "I'll find her for you," he promised as he left.

It was evident to Daniel that although the couple wouldn't take turning over Lucia's care lightly, they were grateful to be doing so. He had passed some kind of test and felt a rush of relief.

Edna was the kind of woman who believed a full stomach helped you think straighter, and she left to bring him a large wedge of apple pie with cheddar cheese mixed right into the crust. Daniel ate it without any real appreciation for the delicious blend of flavors. He only noticed that eating something solid relieved that sloshy sensation in his stomach from all the coffee he'd drunk.

He was halfway through his second mammoth slice when Harvey returned. "She's at Caleb's place," he announced with no preamble.

"That's surprising," his wife answered, and Daniel worried.

"How so?" Harvey responded. Daniel waited for Edna's response, glancing from one to the other nervously. What was wrong with Caleb for crying out loud? Did he need to rush off in some new direction to save Lucia? This could get tiring.

"She needs to get away. She's got to go somewhere." Her father shrugged fatalistically.

"She should have gone south," Edna declared. "If she's gotta get away, she might as well be warm. You know how she hates the cold. She needs more than getting away if she's gone to northern Wisconsin this time of year. She needs her head examined. I know Caleb lets her stay for free during the off-season, but *you get what you pay for* in this case."

"This Caleb," Daniel interjected quickly while he could, "she's safe with him?"

"Is *he* safe with *her* would be more like it."

Daniel panicked. But before his thoughts could go any further, Harvey continued, saving Daniel from giving away his insecurities or insulting their darling paragon's virtues.

"She's got more cussed stubbornness packed into that little pint-size body of hers than any other ten people got a right to," he allowed.

"Pot calling the kettle black," Edna contributed as she swept the booth clear of dishes.

But Harvey ignored his wife for a little man-to-man discussion with Daniel on how best to handle the current situation. "Do you want me to get one of the boys to come take over for me here and go with you to get her?"

Now that was interesting. He'd actually asked Daniel's permission to help in the search-and-retrieve mission. It showed that Harvey was ready to step back and let someone else take over handling Lucia's independence attacks. And from his expression, he seemed quite relieved.

Daniel thought for a solid minute. "It's safe for her up there?"

"Well . . ." Harvey said slowly. "I can't think anything *too* bad could happen to her up at the campgrounds. Caleb stays there year around to keep an eye on the place."

"She's *camping*?" Daniel yelped. And was an eye the only thing good old cousin Caleb was keeping on his Lucia?

"No," Edna assured him. "There are cabins, too."

"Yeah," Harvey agreed. "She's not crazy herself, she'll just drive *you* nuts."

"That's no drive, it's a short putt," Edna quickly contributed.

The woman was starting to fascinate Daniel. Her supply of clichés was truly never-ending. And the deadpan delivery as she dropped each gem was impeccable.

"If she's safe, I'm not going after her," Daniel announced baldly. "She should have the time she says she needs. We just have to trust that she'll come back like she said she would." Her parents looked amazed at his attitude and he grinned at them. "And if it takes her more than two weeks to come to her senses, I'll go up there and drag her home by the roots of her hair."

Harvey laughed and slapped him on the back. "That's the way, son. Like Mom says, *cream will always rise to the top.* You'll do just fine."

He looked slyly at Mrs. Callahan and said, "I'd rather not force her, though, for *a captive heart is a silent bed partner.*" Edna looked decidedly impressed with his use of a cliché she was unfamiliar with herself.

He made a mistake and stretched while yawning. It cost him his trip back home that evening as Edna keyed in on the yawn. Daniel ended by staying overnight so that he could get a fresh start in the morning, for as Edna Callahan was quick to point out, *one couldn't soar with the eagles if one stayed up to hoot with the owls.* Daniel took that to mean he shouldn't drive all night and try to accomplish anything in the morning. His ability to think on his feet had always been a source of pride for him, but he was caught up short and couldn't think of a comeback except the one about burning your candles at both ends, which did nothing to advance *his* side of the argument, so he stayed.

Finally back in the city, he threw himself into his work. His parents called and wanted him to come to Racine for Christmas, but Daniel stayed alone in his apartment, feeling sorry for himself as he rattled around the place. It had grown in size and developed echoes in the corners while he was down in Chillicothe. Daniel hadn't wallowed in self-pity like this since he'd broken his leg in three places in a game of unsupervised tackle football as an eight-year-old.

Finally, midway between Christmas and New Year's, Lucia was back. He could sense it the minute he stepped off the elevator and into his outer office. He entered the inner office just knowing she was there.

And she was. But not to work. She sat in a chair looking out the massive glass wall, studying the cityscape below. She wore a red-and-black-plaid flannel lumberjack shirt with a red turtleneck underneath. Both were tucked into snug jeans and held there with a leather belt. Her feet were encased in low lambs'-wool-lined boots and she looked like an advertisement for a sporting goods store. "Hi," she murmured softly, looking unsure of herself.

"Hi," he breathed back uneasily. He evidently hadn't lost all his business acumen since meeting Lucia. Things just plain felt wrong in the room.

She gave him an awkward little smile that showed nothing of her teeth. "I've been away."

"I know."

She stood to face him and wiped her hands on her jeans before folding them nervously in front of her. "I'm back now."

"So I see." He entered the room more fully, setting his briefcase and topcoat on his desk.

"I needed some time to think things through."

Warily, Daniel responded. "That's what Roseanne said. Come to any earthshaking conclusions?" With an effort at casualness, he walked to the small refrigerator by the built-in bar and poured himself a small orange juice. He held the juice carton up toward her in a silent offer. She shook her head in refusal.

"I guess..." She stopped and took a breath. "I guess you were right, Daniel. You can't buy your way into adulthood with a marriage license. Mom will have to accept that I'm living outside her home before I've snagged a man. If she and Dad can't, I guess that's their problem. I'm okay with it." Lucia was looking all around the room, everywhere in fact, other than directly into Daniel's face. "And maybe I was trying to fill an empty spot I had by campaigning for a husband. Anyway, I called off the husband hunt a long time ago.''

She had?

''To be perfectly honest—''

Daniel braced himself, knowing that any time somebody said ''perfectly honest'' like that, one had better prepare oneself.

''You'll laugh, but I'd hoped . . . I mean, once or twice I thought, maybe *you'd* be interested.'' She gave a pained little smile when Daniel nearly choked on his juice. ''Pretty funny, huh? Well, I guess I've got some growing up to do before I get serious anyway.'' She shrugged her shoulders. ''You're safe. Your company's safe. Everybody's safe all the way around.''

Geez. And he was supposed to be Mr. Perceptive Business Executive. He hadn't had the slightest inkling she'd been considering *him*. He'd wanted her to stop and examine her motives, but now that she'd gone all introspective on him and reached some of the very same conclusions he'd worried over, there was no sense of elation. He felt letdown, ...depressed. Talk about your blue Christmas. Try a blue rest-of-his-life without her. Couldn't they do their growing together? He probably had a little room for improvement himself. He just couldn't think where it might be, offhand.

Lucia turned to go while Daniel was still caught up in his thoughts. Her shoulders were not drooping in defeat. No, she had grown quite a bit already over the long weekend. There was a new serenity about her that Daniel couldn't help but notice. She paused with her hand on the doorknob leading to the outer office. Speaking with evident care, she informed him, ''I turned in my resignation to Roseanne, but she refused to accept it. She wants me to stay and help get the system up when the new computer comes in. If you have any objections to that you'd better

say so now...." She paused. "Well, I guess I'll be in tomorrow. I'm going to unpack and get myself organized the
rest of the day, okay?"

"Hmm? Oh, sure. Sure. That's fine."

Lucia gave him an odd look. He was studying his empty
juice glass as though he had no idea how it had come into
his possession. There was really nothing else to say, so she
mumbled a goodbye and left.

Carefully, Daniel set the glass down on the highly polished desk top and tried to think. What had just happened here, and how was he going to wiggle his way out of
this one?

Just when he was well and truly caught in her web, Lucia decided to go it solo. Wasn't that just like a woman? He
smacked his fist on the desk top, hard, and immediately
regretted it. His eyes narrowed as he shook the painful
appendage. He stood up abruptly and was immediately
attacked by some of the jungle greenery. Viciously, he
knocked it out of his way and stalked over to the refrigerator. He was sorely tempted to go for something stronger
than orange juice, even if it was only nine in the morning.

Forgoing temptation, he poured another glass of orange
juice and sipped through tight lips. He considered his predicament.

Here was his out. Lucia had called off the hunt. All was
well. He was depressed as hell. Somewhere along the line,
he'd stopped worrying about protecting his company from
the little man-eater. He was perfectly willing to throw an
arm or a leg her way, just as long as it was his. He didn't
want to take the out she'd just tossed him. He wanted to
be there for her, protecting her. He wanted her there for
him, breathing fire at her brothers as she did her best to
protect him.

He lowered his frame into the well-constructed chair and
drummed out "The Hike Song" with his fingers on his

desk top. He'd *liked* it when Lucia had finally stood up to her family. And *he'd* been the catalyst. She'd been a tigress, and he knew exactly how she had felt for he'd felt the same way when the street bum had threatened *her*. Surely they could build something lasting on such strong emotions.

There was nothing wrong with Lucia fulfilling a few personal needs were she to get married. So what? What needs was he meeting by going after her now that she'd called off the hunt? To prove he could still get the girl? To fill a freshly discovered empty spot in himself? The past week and a half had been the longest and loneliest of his life. Oh, he knew the old saw about missing a toothache once it was gone, but this was different. Lucia was a shining light that brightened a darkness he hadn't even been aware he'd had.

Maybe Lucia was the perceptive one. At least she'd been aware she *had* an empty spot that needed filling. Well, didn't that beat all?

He slapped the top of the desk, forgetting about his sore hand and making it sting all over again. She wasn't going to get away with this. Punching the intercom, he informed his secretary he would be out for the day and grabbed his coat off the chair where he'd draped it. He ate up the distance between his inner sanctum and the elevator bank in a few very long strides.

Daniel parked his car in a no-parking-here-to-corner zone and wasn't even subtle about it, blatantly blocking the crosswalk. A parking ticket was the least of his worries at this point. Especially if he succeeded in talking Lucia into marrying him.

Lucia didn't answer the door. Daniel panicked. What if she'd gone again? He would burst like a balloon left to swell in the hot sun if he didn't release some of the feelings he was carrying inside. The pressure was mounting in his chest as his emotions built.

He gave up ringing and pounded with his fist instead. Lucia answered on the third round, the vacuum turned off but the hose still in hand.

"Hi," she said, her surprise evident as she stepped back to avoid becoming victim to the next knock and wondered what on God's green earth he was doing there.

Daniel's heart sank. Mr. Big City Executive hadn't thought what to say once he got this far. He bought time with a heart-stopping smile that had Lucia reeling.

"Umm, can I come in?" He frowned. Great, now he was stuttering.

The grimace had Lucia taking another step back. But the correction came automatically. "*May* I come in." It was tough to keep a good education minor on a tight rein, but correcting Daniel's grammar was probably not the brightest thing she'd ever do.

Daniel was so befuddled, he didn't even notice. He simply entered the apartment. Lucia was obviously in the middle of some heavy-duty cleaning. Even in her frazzled-looking state with her hair tied back in a scarf, a truly disreputable shirt tie-dyed in an experiment that must have failed and jeans rolled up to display heavy yellow knit socks and feet jammed into flip-flops, she still looked desirable to him, which only went to show how far his mental state had deteriorated. "Lucia," he announced after clearing his throat. "We need to talk." He walked over and planted himself on her plum sofa.

She hadn't moved from her position by the front door and looked at him a little uncertainly. Surely they'd covered everything in his office? "Okay, Daniel," she said cautiously. "What did you want to talk about?" Just being in the same general vicinity with him excited her, and she promised herself a good biofeedback course to keep her pulse under control around him. She put a hand over her heart in a futile effort to slow its palpitations and looked more closely at Daniel. What was wrong with him? She'd given him everything he wanted, hadn't she? But he looked upset instead of relieved, which made no sense at all unless...

Daniel jumped off the sofa and began pacing. His hands were clasped behind his back and he looked like a bad imitation of Groucho Marx. "Lucia," he finally announced. "It's time we took a closer look at this relationship of ours." He raised his sights from the rug to make sure he had her undivided attention. "Get rid of the vacuum and sit down, Lu, you're making me nervous standing there like that. Vacuuming can wait for a minute." It was damn right it could wait. She could at least look interested when his whole future hung in the balance.

Lucia dropped the hose where she stood and sat, clearly too taken aback by his behavior to argue. Daniel nodded in satisfaction. "Now I've given this a lot of thought...."

It was difficult to do any real pacing in such a small area, but Daniel managed somehow. "I realize I'm not exactly what you were looking for in a man. I'm a little taller than you wanted and I do tend to be a bit more directive than you'd care for...."

Lucia's eyebrows rose in amazement at Daniel's personality analysis—a *little* taller? A *bit* too directive?

"But it's a misconception about not being able to teach old dogs new tricks. I can learn."

Daniel continued, pleased with the cliché he'd thrown into his speech. He was certain it was an omen about his ability to fit into her family that it had come so easily. "I can adapt. But you'll have to as well." He pointed an accusing finger at her. Lucia's hands immediately flew to her chest in a "what, who me?" gesture. "You're not exactly what *I* was looking for, either. Not that I was looking at all, you understand," he added quickly.

"People don't pick on you just because you're short, you know. Some of the things you do are genuinely goofy."

So she would get counseling.

"You're so short I get a backache trying to kiss you and we look silly walking together."

Maybe stilts were coming into fashion.

He studied her a moment. "You won't make me a very good corporate wife."

Hey, now. She'd thrown a pretty good company Christmas party and hadn't used the wrong fork even once.

"You keep yourself so busy with all your pet projects we'd have to make appointments to see each other if you maintained them all."

Oh, yeah? Well, what trees had he planted that he could criticize hers so freely?

Daniel could tell by her lowering brow that he wasn't on the right track. He plopped down beside her and sighed tiredly, rubbing his eyes. "I'm not doing this very well, am I?"

He tried again. "Here's the thing, Lu. Logically, we're all wrong for each other. But logical or not, you and I make sparks fly."

Oh, yes. Yes, they surely did.

"I know I've accused you of all kinds of ulterior motives in this husbandly pursuit of yours, some of which were probably right on the money. But big deal."

Yeah, big deal.

"When I think about it, my own motives for *not* wanting to get married and then pursuing you anyway are not the most rational. And you know what they say about people living in glass houses."

Her mom had mentioned them in passing once or twice.

"The thing is, down deep I know we've got what it takes to make it work. And logical or not, we owe it to ourselves to give it our best shot." He reached over and took her hand. "What do you think?"

What did she think? She thought caution was unfortunately the order of the day. Daniel had yet to mention one very important item. "Possibly."

Daniel looked at her oddly. "Lucia, you're speaking in single words. Have you forgotten how to string a sentence together?"

So now *she* spoke in phrases, and Daniel's clichés were as plentiful as popcorn on a movie theater floor. Well, *what went around came around*, her mother would say.

"Daniel," she declared. "I love you. I have for some time."

Daniel was floored, thrilled and finally confused in quick succession. "Then why not a 'yes' instead of 'possibly'?"

"I just said I love you, but you have yet to mention anything having to do with your feelings on this subject. The entire conversation has revolved around a potential marriage's workability and logic." She gave him a stubborn look and pulled her hand away from his. "I want to know if you love me. None of the rest of the stuff really matters one way or another if you do."

Reaching over, he pulled her onto his lap and kissed her soundly. "I love you," he admitted. "And since none of the rest of the stuff matters, we're getting married as soon as possible and have lots of babies for you to buy lunch boxes and crayons for in the fall and dress in froufrou Easter hats every spring."

He'd remembered. She kissed him back and was a goner.

"For want of a nail, the battle was lost," he whispered.

"Beg pardon?"

"Only in our case, it should be 'for want of a screw-driver, their hearts were lost.'"

She fought her way through the sensual fog descending around her. "Hmm? *Oh*, you're talking about the baby buggy episode."

"I'm talking about the baby buggy episode," he concurred. "And when we fill *our* baby buggy, we're going to let that sleeping baby lie."

"Dogs," she murmured against his lips. "That's let sleeping *dogs* lie."

"Don't like dogs," he returned. "We're going to have babies, not dogs. And we're not going to wake them up when they're sleeping, either. Your mother would approve."

"She's going to adore having you for a son-in-law," Lucia confided, before kissing him with such fervor and hunger that he was left platitude-less for some time to come.

*   *   *   *   *

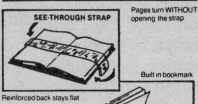

Silhouette Intimate Moments®

NORA ROBERTS
brings you the first
Award of Excellence title
Gabriel's Angel
coming in August from
Silhouette Intimate Moments

They were on a collision course with love....

Laura Malone was alone, scared—and pregnant. She was running for the sake of her child. Gabriel Bradley had his own problems. He had neither the need nor the inclination to get involved in someone else's.

But Laura was like no other woman ... and she needed him. Soon Gabe was willing to risk all for the heaven of her arms.

The Award of Excellence is given to one specially selected title per month. Look for the second Award of Excellence title, coming out in September from Silhouette Romance—**SUTTON'S WAY** by **Diana Palmer**

Im 300-1